JENNY FABIAN

was brought up in a b
school. 'She was perfe
until she was four yea
mother. After writing
Chemical Romance she
country to recover. She recently returned
to London and is writing again.

A Chemical Romance

Romance

Jenny Fabian

THE DO-NOT
PRESS

First Published in Great Britain in 1971 by Talmy, Franklin Ltd
This edition published in 1998 by
The Do-Not Press
PO Box 4215
London SE23 2QD

ISBN 1 899344 42 X

British Library Cataloguing in Publication Data. A catalogue
record for this book is available from the British Library.

h g f e d c b a

Printed and bound in Great Britain by The Guernsey Press Co Ltd.

DEDICATED TO NEAL PHILLIPS WHO DIED OF A
DRUG OVERDOSE ON A STREET IN BOMBAY.

Author's Introduction

The girl who wrote *Groupie* became the girl who wrote about the girl who wrote *Groupie*. Muddled? She certainly was. One interviewer remarked: 'There seem to be more of you than there are of me.'

After the great baring of bodies came the great baring of souls. Full of mind-expanding drugs, everything had to have a meaning, especially for us chicks. We were trying to fight our way out of the kitchen, and looking for guys who loved us for our minds as well as for our bodies. The days of sitting on a cushion rolling joints for rock-gods in between blow jobs was coming to an end.

Before writing *Groupie* with Johnny Byrne I was just another chick with a Bob Dylan poster on my wall. I'd been swept off my feet by a poet called Spike Hawkins, who turned me on, and I felt as though I was floating out of my body. After that, I never wanted to be any other way; I wanted to be more so. Syd Barrett's music did that for me. *Groupie* was born.

A Chemical Romance is a bridge between the girl in *Groupie* and the girl who had written it. The meaning of status has shifted; status by association has become status through achievement. Nowadays we're used to the identity crisis inevitably suffered by the too-much-too-soon people – it goes with the job. But in the days of early freak-dom, people in the headlines were divided by the good and the upright or the slag-heap known as the *News of the World*. The media saw me as shock/horror copy, and I was too stoned to argue my corner. There were other forces at work, like the world of Mammon insidiously destroying my working relationship with Johnny Byrne, and the constant intangible, love.

I had to get away from the casual celebrity-land rela-tionships, and thought that a rose-covered cottage up Laurel Canyon with a dysfunctional guitarist might be the answer. But like Bonnie and Clyde, I wasn't heading nowhere, I was running from. So me and my alter-ego flew to Ibiza, early communal paradise for back-to-nature living and nothing to worry about except the joys of troil-ism and how high can you get? The answer is tantalisingly close.

During the writing of *A Chemical Romance* I was living in a commune of writers in a house previously occupied by members of the Bloomsbury Set. It was full of literary ghosts and disembodied spirits, as well as a never-ending supply of LSD, cocaine, pot and Mandrax. I may whinge about how the whole thing of it drove me to madness and self-destruction, but I had a great time getting there. *A Chemical Romance* is part of the journey.

– *Jenny Fabian, London 1998*

1

'Mason is having a party and we're invited,' Jay told me.

'Did he ask me, I mean, me specifically?' I asked.

'Not exactly, but I told him about the book we'd written and suggested this as a preliminary meeting before we get down to office tactics.'

'There'll be lots of glamorous people there. What on earth shall I wear?'

'Anything you like. Something transparent.'

So I put on my 1920's red chiffon tube with coloured beads dotted in just enough places to be discreet and nervously followed Jay in Mason's penthouse, all prepared to be impressed.

'There's Mason,' said Jay, and I saw a young superman standing surrounded by bosomy girls in low-cut dresses. I suddenly felt extremely flat and shapeless in my tube and slightly unsuitable.

'Here she is, Mason, here's Tiptree,' and Mason looked half at me through rosy shades, half at Jay, half smiled and half extended his hand.

'I hear you've written a book with Jay that's got lots of sex in it,' he said, in a quiet American voice. He looked over my shoulder and I nervously turned round in case there were two of me before I managed to say yes. Jay had warned me he was virtually blind but pretended he wasn't and didn't like people to know.

'Well, I'd like to read it.'

'Oh, yes.'

'Perhaps next week?'

'Yes.'

And that was that. I spent the rest of the evening staring at all the overdressed and overexposed chicks, the smooth looking guys and Mason. For all his myopic vision, he seemed quite normal. I wondered how this could be, how could he fill his house with all these people to trip over and bump into, how could he be such a successful agent, a crafty business man who couldn't look you in the eye? He had an internal agent, I decided, that gave off power vibes. He had zapped me with his power. I wanted him to like the book and wanted him to like me. And I wanted him to make me rich and famous.

Before we showed the book to Mason, Jay had another card to play. He wanted an outside opinion, just to know what we'd got up our sleeves. So, looking like a couple of overdressed tourists, we went to meet a publishing editor who had read our manuscript.

'Do you think they'll say it's incredible, fantastic, how much do you want, anything you say, definite best-seller?' I asked Jay.

'I doubt it,' he replied. 'Even though they may be thinking it.'

'Could they think something like that about it?'

'We do, don't we?'

'If you believe in miracles.'

'Of course.'

'Lets hope everyone does.'

Mr Michael Sandman came into the reception to meet us. I had my protective nonchalance in operation and found myself sitting in my first publishers' office without it having any effect. The book covers pinned round the wall looked unfamiliar and uninteresting. The furniture had G-plan negativity. The desk was made of cheap wood and the phone looked like a plastic toy. The young Mr Sandman was not long out of university and looked like Prince Charles. He paused to decide that we were a couple of average hippies before he cautiously showed us into his office.

'It's unpublishable,' he stated.

I stood up to leave.

'What do you mean?' demanded Jay, ignoring me and leaning back in his chair.

'As it stands, it's unpublishable,' Sandman repeated.

'What's wrong with it?' Jay asked.

I shrugged and sat down, though I wasn't interested. Now it was finished I could never change a word.

'It's unbelievable. It doesn't ring true.'

Jay and I exchanged the first of many knowing smiles.

'Meaningless fiction?' Jay inquired quizzically.

'There's very little plot and not enough explanation of where all these people came from and what made them the way they are.'

'Exactly. That's how it is.'

Mr Sandman didn't understand. Neither did I.

'Doesn't it sound real at all?' I asked. 'Do you think we made it all up?'

'Don't tell me there's a *real* Katie,' Mr Sandman gave a cynical grin. 'Nobody in their right mind would behave like that.'

'So I'm not in my right mind,' I murmured to myself, and Mr Sandman looked at me sharply.

'Surely reality isn't so important,' Jay said, still not ready to reveal all, 'as long as a book holds the attention and entertains.'

'We demand slightly more of our books than that.' Mr Sandman looked stern. 'We have to consider the quality of the writing and the interest value of the story. Your book is very limited.'

'Deliberately so,' replied Jay. 'It's concentrating on one

particular way of life to the exclusion of all outside elements except when they intrude into her private world.'

'But you can't just deny majority existence. She doesn't even think of things outside the pop world.'

'The pop world is her majority existence. Nothing else has any meaning.'

'But she doesn't even seem to think she's doing anything unusual. She never compares herself to other girls.'

'Except those living the same way as she does. It's deliberate, I assure you.'

I couldn't stand it any longer. I would sacrifice my secret to help Mr Sandman understand.

'Would you like to know why it's deliberate?' I demanded. 'Because it's true. I mean, the girl is me and the musicians are real and so are the situations. We've just brought in the necessary inaccuracies to call it fiction. We thought it was quite funny.'

Mr Sandman stared at me.

'Does it shock you?' asked Jay.

'Not me,' he said boldly. 'But it might shock W.H. Smith.'

Jay shrugged. 'But did *you* enjoy it, without worrying about the W.H. Smith brigade?'

'It's slightly crude,' Mr Sandman admitted.

'So are pop musicians,' I commented.

'But other things,' Mr Sandman turned on me questioningly. 'Those scenes in the office, for example, surely that never really happened? Things like that certainly don't happen in this office.' He laughed.

'Would you like them to?' asked Jay.

'I can't say I've thought about it. It's rather indiscreet and I don't see the point.'

'But you did see the point in the book?' Jay probed.

'It didn't do her much good.'

'And isn't it interesting that it didn't do her any harm, either?'

'Perhaps. So what was the point of it?'

Jay paused, and I felt he wanted me to explain. But I was too absorbed in listening about myself in the third person to think about a long-gone Why. Anyway, Jay was better at explaining me than I was.

'She's a chick who'll put herself through all kinds of situations to get what she wants. Whether she wins or loses isn't the point. The point is her motivation and the unfamiliar rules she's applying. And sometimes it's easier to do something you don't want that to irritate someone with rigid morals when all he needs is a plate.'

'Yes, a plate,' murmured Mr Sandman. 'You've got a lot of plates in your book. Are you using the word as a noun or a verb?'

'More of a moving gesture,' Jay quipped, and I giggled.

'A new kind of slang?'

'Surely the meaning is obvious?'

'Perhaps I call it something else,' Mr Sandman might have been getting embarrassed.

'Like what?' I demanded.

'I'm sure *you* know *all* the expressions, Miss Gibbon, being such an experienced lady. Perhaps you could give me your version of plating.'

'Perhaps I should show you,' I said, 'but things like that don't happen in offices like this where there isn't any point in being indiscreet, do they?' I paused. 'Do you understand?'

He did, and his face reddened with confusion.

'There's an awful lot of it in your book.'

'But nobody's written about it at all before.'

'Has anyone else read this?' Mr Sandman indicated our manuscript.

'You're the first,' Jay told him and watched carefully.

'I'd like to hang on to it for a while, to get a few more opinions, you know. Biographical details about both of you would be a help as well.'

'You'll have to see my agent about both those things. That's our only copy and he'll be needing it.'

'Who's your agent?' Mr Sandman was surprised.

'Mason Radar.'

Mr Sandman gave us both a sharp look and accepted the card Jay handed him almost reluctantly.

'I see ...' he said slowly, but he never saw us again, for Mason had his own plans. Before we'd finished reading the book to him he was talking about contracts and percentages and laughing his head off. I stopped trembling at his feet and he offered me a drink.

I accepted a brimming glass of something red and watched him muttering through the intercom. He glittered behind silver-rimmed Joe Cools, and round his neck hung the magic symbol of Horus, the all-seeing eye in the mouth of the sun. By the time the contract appeared I felt a bit more confident and argued about a clause. Mason had it re-written so that I didn't understand it, and I signed happily, for whatever it meant in print, it meant money to me. And money bought me time to do nothing except enjoy myself and turn my head inside out. I had to hang around a lot while Jay fussed and fumed over clauses and conditions but I found it far easier just to put all my trust in Mason. Wasn't that what I was paying him his percentage for? Jay said he was just checking, and I didn't mind because I thought he might as well, for I wasn't much use. I didn't have to work any more and enjoyed going to Mason's office very stoned and watching all the activity without having to do anything. I was smoking a lot of dope, buying a lot of clothes, looking for somewhere better to live, and waiting for the book to come out.

2

I'd seen Dr P. Atmos around for some time, lounging about dimly-lit luxurious pads that had recently become part of my circuit. We hadn't spoken to each other, and I wasn't sure if he was a *real* doctor or a pretend one. But if he was a real doctor, he looked like the kind of doctor who'd know what I needed, and I went along to see him.

The modern block of flats with net curtains and midget porters all looked pretty real. I was shown into a large square room by a blonde girl in a hurry. The walls were draped and fringed, and the low ceiling was frescoed. The floor was covered in cushions and the round table was littered with planets and stars. Indian music, joss sticks; yet in spite of it all I liked it.

Then Dr Atmos was all around me, peering through his long hair and pulling on a sports jacket over his silver Lurex t-shirt. He told me to hang on a minute and disappeared through a velvet wall. A moment later he beckoned me into his surgery. I sat in a basket hanging from the ceiling while he rummaged in his bureau for a card. There were shawls draped everywhere and witty advertisements for laxatives and contraceptives, tranquillisers and analgesics. On top of his bureau were three multi-coloured phones, a cash register and a statue of Buddha. Dr P Atmos was into blowing people's minds before he started treating their heads.

'What's your birth sign?' he asked, pen poised above the card with my name at the top.

'Gemini.'

'Rising sign?'

'Don't really know.' He looked at me seriously.

'Time of birth?' He looked hopefully at the cosmic calendar above his desk.

'Sorry, I'll have to ask my mother.'

'Shall we do that now?' he suggested.

'If you like,' I said, and wondered what she'd think.

'I like to have an Astroflash done on all my patients,' he explained.

'That's nice,' I said, 'though I've only come for some sleepers.'

'Grooving or sleeping?' he asked.

'A bit of both,' I replied. 'What do I pay you?

He handed me a prescription and rang up the cash register. It said 'No Sale'.

'That's very kind of you,' I said.

'I hear you have a book coming out – perhaps you'd like to sign me a copy?' he suggested, and I offered him a proof copy.

'Bring it round for supper next week and collect your Astroflash,' he suggested.

Next week the same chick answered the door and this time she almost smiled.

'This is Alice,' Atmos introduced us.

I supposed she was his lady; she cooked the supper and lay around looking possessive. She had a wide-eyed windswept look and a long flat body. Spread out of the cushions she could have been an abandoned mermaid, a wood nymph, a fairy queen, a small-time goddess...

'Actually, I'm Queen Guinevere at the moment,' she piped. 'And I'd like to be a movie star.' Her accent was well-bred and I though she was very daring and imaginative for a bourgeois.

After the brown rice crumble Atmos read my Astroflash

out loud. It told me all these things I knew about myself and Alice twittered excitedly.

'I've got endless planets in Gemini,' she explained, 'so I'm very much the same as you.'

They were very inquisitive about my life, and seemed to like me so much they offered me a room in their flat when they found out my housing problem.

'We had a young Honourable living here,' Atmos explained, 'but he's gone searching out East for a while. So we need someone else.'

'My agent says I can't be living in a rock group's house when the publicity starts, though I'd have thought it rather suitable. But I might as well live somewhere comfortable now I can afford it and this looks ready-made.'

I was delighted with my square white room and decided to make it symmetrical and Japanese with everything on the floor. For the first time I took some care with my environment. I was already into Image. The young Honourable had left behind some tasty Eastern hangings which fitted in with my scheme, and lots of heavy Eastern reading that I intended to investigate. I'd given Zen a miss in '67 and felt a gap in my philosophy.

For the next few months I lay on the cushions getting stoned inside the headphones and watching Atmos and Alice playing games with each other. There were a lot of quarrels in the kitchen as Alice hated cooking because she felt she was missing interesting conversations and all the joints. She often lost her temper and cried, accusing Atmos of treating her like a slave. She reckoned that rushing around in a wig and padded bra auditioning for commercials was much harder work that looking up girls' snatches all day long, and that the cooking should be shared equally.

If she got too aggressive, Atmos would send her away and different ladies would come to visit and care for him. Although I wasn't much interested in fish and vegetables I often made an effort to help Alice in the kitchen. Then she could complain to me about the trauma of liberation from her background and expose the gruesome problems of being in love with a Scorpio. I had no Scorpios on my record to compare with Atmos, only a few Capricorns, Leos and Geminis, and they were complicated enough. I noticed that Alice was much more physical than me; when she wasn't entwining herself around Atmos with love in her eyes, she would be hitting him and throwing things at him with tears in her eyes. There could be high drama at any moment over anything, and I watched fascinated as they blatantly insisted on performing their soap opera in front of me. In the beginning, being outside it all, it was a farce to be laughed at. But slowly, inexorably, I was drawn in as the three-sided friendship developed. Alice had read my story, peering over the top of it from time to stare at me; I couldn't decide whether in outrage or admiration.

'Too much,' she said once, putting down the book and staring. 'Too much.'

'What's that?' I inquired.

'I loved an American freak called Larry too,' she said. 'I met him when I was a Bluebell dancer and he used to go into Central Park and talk to the statues.'

'I'm going to America one day to find my Larry again,' I said, 'because I believe he was something special.'

'Mine was,' she said. 'I lived with him for a year until I couldn't stand it any longer. He was too freaked out, so I had to get on a plane and come home. He just said "alright, baby". He took so much dope he's probably dead by now.'

'Mine went mad and got shut in a nut bin,' I said. 'He sometimes writes me letters in capital letters. He believes in cosmic love and destiny.'

'Of course,' Alice agreed. 'My Larry was like that too. He said I was his anima come to life and I thought that was beautiful. It made me feel hermaphroditic.'

She looked at me meaningfully, for it was down in black and white that I had enjoyed another lady, and she was still baulking. Atmos was constantly trying to pressure her into threesomes, but it was too emotionally complicated for her, and it always reached a point where fear got the better of her, and she would run out of their bedroom in a frenzy, crying 'I'm not freaking out, I'm not freaking out', and dash into my bedroom and pour out the details of her non-adventure.

I was starting to find Alice attractive and wondered whether to try and be the first. But Atmos was a complication. He had his own plans to get me into bed with or without Alice. He would send Alice to bed and then make a pot of tea for two, turning down the sounds and putting up the pressure. His seductive mind would lead the conversation round to sexual liberation.

'I'm a hundred percenter living thirty years ahead of my time,' he said confidentially, putting his hand on my knee, 'and I can tell that you are too.'

'Sometimes,' I said cautiously.

'Sure you are,' he insisted, 'more than Alice is.'

'She feels a hundred percent about you.'

'But her repressions hold her back in so many things.'

'I've got anal repressions,' I told him hopefully, thinking it might put him off. 'So I can't be a hundred percenter.'

'Anal repression?' Atmos sounded shocked. 'You'll be needing to get rid of that.'

'I've had it for a long time.'

'Too long, I should say,' Atmos stated.

'I'm waiting for the right moment.'

'I cured Alice.'

'I'll know when the right moment comes.'

'Why not take a chance?'

'I'm not ready.'

'That's no excuse,' and Atmos put his face close to mine. I moved back and picked up my cup of tea to try and hide my embarrassment.

'I'm not after your anal repression,' Atmos joked. 'I just love you anyway.' He moved in again.

'I love you too,' I felt forced to say, and looked straight ahead. I could feel him moving in again. I stopped him.

'What about Alice?' I asked feebly.

'She loves you too.'

All this talk of love confused me since I had spent the last couple of years learning not to mention the word. I supposed Atmos meant it in a more general way.

'It upsets her to think of us sleeping together,' I told him. 'She knows you want to and is trying not to let it interfere with our friendship. But I don't want to hurt her, and I don't think you should confuse her.'

'She loves being confused.'

'Well, I don't and this is quite a confusing situation.'

'If you see it that way. I just see it as something nice between friends.'

'But because we're friends and we love each other anyway, there doesn't seem to be any *need*.'

Atmos gave me an exasperated look.

'You're talking in circles,' he said.

'I don't like being pressured,' I replied.

He drew back and looked at me in mock alarm.

'Have I gone too far?' he asked over-anxiously. 'Oh, I have! I've gone too far again,' and he slapped himself on the knee, rebuking himself. I had to laugh, but also had to escape to bed before he went too far again.

Alice had already quarrelled with Atmos about his attempts to seduce me. She lay in bed imagining things.

'What can I do with him?' she wailed. 'He wants to poke it into every chick in the world.'

'It's his ego,' I suggested.

'What about it?' she demanded.

'It's too big.'

'Sometimes I think so too,' she agreed sadly. 'Sometimes I'm tempted to jet-set off with some movie producer to Gstaad and get discovered. I'm sure I'm meant to be a star, it's just that I find all those numbers so hard to go through with now. It was different when my hair was long and I wore mini-skirts; guys used to take me seriously. Now they think I'm crazy and just laugh at me.'

I could see nothing wrong in that, and suggested she gave it a try even if only to make Atmos take some notice.

'I think I'll make a phone call,' she said. 'There's this fucked-up movie guy who wants me to mother him; that's always good for a mind-blow.'

But he wasn't in for two weeks, and meanwhile the soap opera continued.

3

'How strongly do you feel about having your name on the cover?' the young publishing editor asked Jay, over the obligatory lunch.

Jay didn't seem to understand, and looked at me in confusion. It was the first remark that made me pay attention and we'd already finished the main course.

'We thought that just Tiptree's name and picture on the cover, making it obvious it's her story, would bring more publicity and more sales. Best-selling lady authors are hard to come by these days, you know.' Another college graduate tuned in to hard sell whatever the cost.

'I feel very strongly about having my name on the cover. We share everything equally.' Jay was insulted, and expected me to back him up.

'I couldn't possibly take full responsibility for the book,' I said, 'and I can see no reason to leave Jay's name off the cover.'

Re-assured, Jay could then be magnanimous.

'I realise that Tiptree is the immediate interest and the publicity angle, but to dismiss me entirely, to make me disown something I helped to create, I'm afraid that's asking too much.'

The editor bowed his thatched head in acquiescence. No more would be said about it. But it was a hint of things to come.

When the publicity started, just before publication, it was me they wanted to interview, it was me they wanted to misquote, it was me they wanted to pass their moral judgement on. I started chugging through three or four interviews a day, arranged through Mason's office and usually without Jay. He went frantic trying to keep up with my appointments, assuming that any interview arranged with me meant him as well. Mason hired a young publicity man who took me aside and suggested I stopped telling Jay about interviews.

'They're not interested in him, you know, and quite frankly, neither am I. Why don't you just tell them he's a ghost writer?'

'I can't believe you,' I said, 'how could you expect me to do that?'

'Easily, if you had any sense. Think of your future. You could be made on your own.'

'Future? I'm afraid the present needs all my attention right now. To have to deal with something as emotional as that would blow it.'

'What?'

'My mind, I mean. It's feeling pretty fragile and sensitive, with all those people looking at it so critically.'

To read about myself sounding so unfamiliar was causing me an identity crisis. I felt I wasn't making myself understood. The questions were boring and stupid, because the book should have told them everything. Endlessly I tried to explain what a groupie was. In just one paragraph. I asked myself questions and wrote down the answers. I tried to be facetious and they took me seriously. I tried to be serious and they felt sorry for me. I was a dirty little girl, a social revelation, a right-wing fascist, a sign-of-the-times gone wrong; funny, boring, sexy, sad, they all saw me differently until I couldn't see myself.

I complained to Mason that the reporters were taking

advantage of me and asking me dirty questions. They were even asking me to pose in the nude. Mason looked amused.

'I'm sure you can give them a dirty answer,' he said.

'No, I'm finding it distasteful,' I insisted. 'This guy from the *Standard* asked me whether I masturbated or not. And that's not for publication, is it?'

I felt Mason should protect me more. I was burning my brain out answering questions and he didn't seem to notice.

'Really,' I insisted, 'I'm not that blasé.'

'I know.' He laughed. 'You used to be the most paranoid chick I'd ever known.'

'Oh, that's terrible,' I said, feeling extremely paranoid.

'Don't worry, you're getting much better. But if you like, I'll sit in on your interviews. You've got one tomorrow and you can have it in the conference room.'

I was getting a father complex about Mason. He was like a super-daddy, giving me money, making me famous, protecting me from con men and defending my interests. I wanted him to take me in his arms and kiss me and tell me how good I was like my father had never done. But his orbit was so much higher than mine and I felt like a tiresome child. And I was too small and dark for him to think of me in any other context. Beautiful blondes. They were Mason's weakness. He'd married his mother in a dark intelligent girl who looked after him just like his mother had, knowing his head and bearing his children, and lying beside him in bed screaming in silence: 'Fuck me,' she had pleaded silently, 'fuck me!' But he hadn't felt like it any more, so she went away and left him to the blondes.

'Why don't you ever go with dark-haired chicks?' I asked him.

'Because I married one,' he retorted, and I wondered if he noticed that next day my hair turned red.

My interview in the conference room was early in the morning. This was a personal conference room in Mason's penthouse above his offices, and I crept up shyly to look for him. There didn't seem to be anyone in his bedroom, so I cautiously went in to investigate his privacy. When I looked towards the far wall I could see straight into Mason's bathroom. It was like a picture on the wall, framed in decorative carved wood, until I realised it was a two-way mirror. The bathroom was almost half the size of the bedroom, the bath itself was a double-headed silver fish, a mouth for hot and a mouth for cold. An uncoiled serpent rose up over the bath with a multi-pronged tongue to provide showering. The tiles on the walls were a mosaic of mermaids, and bright green Astroturf lined the floor. The ceiling was a glowing square of diffused light, and amongst all this Pisces in Aquarius I could see Mason, dressed in a towelling toga, peering at himself in a neon-lit mirror above the marble basin and reaching for his electric razor. But he'd picked up a small transistor radio, and as he held it to his face, Jimmy Young came booming out with the morning's recipe. Mason looked alarmed and shouted for Lombard, his valet. I got scared and left the bedroom.

The interview had already started by the time Mason entered, looking starched and pressed in a maroon suit and black patent boots. He nodded vaguely in our direction and carefully took a discreet seat at the far end of the room. He lit a cigarette and settled back, his shades pointing straight at me, thick and black, and again I wondered how much he could see. I started feeling uneasy under his scrutiny, and tried extra-hard to give good answers. I felt him criticising the way I handled myself. I was answering for him as well as the reporter, and creaking under the double strain. After half-an-hour a phone rang and Mason reached for it. A few mumbled words, then carefully replacing the receiver, he got up.

'Excuse me,' he said, and walked convincingly towards the door.

'Who was *that*?' demanded the reporter.

'That's my agent,' I said.

Having Mason lurking in the corner during interviews didn't seem to help, so the experiment was dropped. Another one was about to start. To cope with the unreality of what was happening I had started dropping acid every day. This made it easy for me to say anything that came into my head and also gave me a false energy to deal with those earthy newspapermen. As I didn't know who I was anyway, I thought I might as well distort my identity at the same time. Jay thought I was crazy and needed help. I agreed, and told him what the publicity man had suggested. There was a furious row in the office between Jay, Mason and the publicity man which resulted in Jay coming to all future interviews. That was quite a relief, because Jay had so much to say, he'd worked out his answers long ago and trotted them out convincingly and enthusiastically. I could pipe up occasionally, but most of the time I sat in a limbo, just waiting for the interview to finish and hoping I hadn't said anything stupid. Let Jay be positive and objective; I'd done my bit long ago. At last he was happy, basking in this weird limelight, at last he could be recognised for what he had created.

He was still having to fight for it, though. The same thing happened when the television interviews started, and I was still being referred to as the sole author. I'd got past caring, and shut my ears to his nagging. I suppose he got his own back when he finally did his first solo interview. He was so excited he had to ring me up, waking me from a very late night, and read it over the phone.

'Thrifty middle-class attitude to money and an efficient typist,' I heard in my ear.

'She taped me a few stories and I made them into a book,' came next, and I burst into tears and slammed down the phone. I hated him for getting at me in such a petty way. I felt disdainful about his betrayal, about his lies. He was pathetic. I didn't want to speak to him or see him for at least two days. I stayed in my Eastern cocoon with the warmth of Atmos and Alice, who seemed to love me more and more as I became crazier and crazier. Alice had told me she had slept with Mason once because she had thought he could get her into movies.

'But my tits were too small and his cock was too large so it didn't really happen,' she said. 'He's into bum-fucking, you know.' My heart sank over the problem of my anal virginity.

'Why don't you ever take *me* out to dinner?' I demanded of Mason as I heard him arranging suitable female escorts for some visiting millionaires.

'Darling, it hadn't occurred to me,' he said. 'I thought you only ate brown rice.'

'Of course I don't,' I replied indignantly. 'That was ages ago.'

'Alright, come to Lucia's tomorrow night.'

Lucia's was exclusive to breadheads, movieheads, statusheads, and all the groupies that went with that kind of scene. Very different from the chicks down the Speakeasy; older, coarser and generally more tasteless, I decided, and much more plastic. I was picked up by Lombard in the Pontiac Firebird and my heart sank to see Cheryl, Mason's current blonde screw, sitting all over Mason in the back seat. We were joined in the bar of Lucia's by two other couples, and everyone knew everyone except me. Mason sat me next to himself at dinner and talked to me about sex.

'I like girls who give good blow-jobs,' he confided in me. 'Cheryl over there,' he lowered his voice, 'well, she'll go down on me, but she won't swallow.'

'That's no good,' I said knowingly. 'What does she do with it then? Rush to the bathroom and spit it out?'

'Something like that.'

'Well, I go down and I swallow,' I told him encouragingly, and watched him stub his cigarette out in the butter dish. Everyone pretended not to notice.

'I can't stand chicks with smelly cunts,' he continued, 'too many chicks have smelly cunts. I like to go down on a chick, but I've got a very sensitive nose and can't stand the slightest odour. You'd be surprised how many chicks have smelly cunts.'

'How horrible,' I said, 'don't they wash? I'm very fond of sitting on the bidet.'

Then I rubbed my finger up my snatch, dipped it in my fruit drink for good measure, and held it under Mason's nose.

'That's my smell,' I told him.

'Very nice,' he said, taken by surprise, and asked for the menu. He pretended to read it and I stared at all the famous people I didn't recognise staring at each other. They were staring at me too, wondering what a hapless hippy was doing in Lucia's. Especially when my hair wasn't blonde and my tits were too small. I felt mis-shapen and misplaced, and reached for the comfort of my sleeping rag.

4

I insisted that the publication party was held in the Speakeasy. I just couldn't bear the thought of the plastic Revolution. In the beginning I found myself standing all alone with nobody to talk to. Jay had already introduced himself to some important-looking suits and the string quartet was just tuning up.

'Have a drink, duckie,' said one of the uniformed waitresses hired for the occasion. 'You'd better come and join us. We're having more of a party than you are.'

'Maybe I'll do that, there's nobody much here,' I said, and took an orange juice. I never mixed alcohol and acid since the time a crepe chiffon blouse had turned into withered skin.

Then a young guy with a beard came up and told me who I was, and although I didn't have anything to say to him I stood near him to look as though I wasn't alone. Then suddenly there were people I knew, people I was supposed to know, people being introduced to me, people with suits who all looked the same but who were supposed to be important, and then Mason, groping his way through the bodies to find me.

'Here I am,' I said, as he pushed past me, 'in case you wondered.'

'Ah, there you are, come with me and meet some people.'

'Where are they?'

'Over there,' and Mason gestured vaguely in the direction he had come from.

'Do I know them?'

'It's the head of Columbia and a vice-president of Metro.'

I tried to spot a likely couple of bigwigs as I pushed my way through with Mason attached to the band of my long T-shirt. There were lots of musician friends there who yelled friendly insults at me until finally a small greasy man reached out an arm, and there I was again talking to suits with nothing to say. I smiled my smiles, shook my hand, said my lines, laughed at theirs and looked for an opening to make my excuses.

'*Fan*tastic, Tiptree Gibbon, how gorgeous to see you,' and a hand slipped round my waist and I turned to look into the crooked smile of Oscar Peel, famous wallaby prankster. He edited *Buzz*, an underground political porno-rag, and had a fast-talking flippant seduction routine that came out automatically to any chick he talked to, accompanied by a lot of nudges and winks. He also had long soft hair that swung into his liquid-brown eyes, and a slender body with a neat bottom.

'*In*credible, you're a star, all those months behind that cash register in the Other Kingdom certainly paid off, now I understand why you never noticed me, perhaps it's not too late to ask you out to dinner?'

'Tonight?' I said.

He stared at me for a moment. 'Why not?' he answered. 'Oh, please excuse me, perhaps you have five appointments with seven directors in six expensive restaurants,' he indicated the suits who had paused politely at his intrusion, 'but I'm very handy with bacon and eggs.'

'What about a restaurant?' I asked.

'Well, I'm sure you're only used to the best, and I'm a poor underground writer. I can offer you a bistro in Notting Hill Gate that serves avocados, however.'

'Perfect,' I replied, and wanted to leave immediately. I turned to Mason and the film magnates.

'So I'm off,' I announced. 'I've been here long enough, haven't I?' I asked Mason. He smiled wanly.

'I'm sure we all have,' he said.

'You sound tired,' I said, and leaned forward and kissed him. Then I turned back to Oscar, and we moved into the crowd, his hand busily exploring the outside of my T-shirt.

'I hope the way I've kidnapped you will stir the romantic in you,' Oscar murmured in my ear, as we passed Jay busily impressing some sixteen-year-olds.

'I must just speak to my friends,' I said, seeing Alice fluttering through the crowd.

'I'm leaving now,' I told her.

'Are we all going to eat somewhere?' she asked.

'Alice, this is Oscar.'

'The lovely Alice Hornby,' Oscar exclaimed. 'I've seen you drinking Lucozade on the telly.'

Alice giggled.

'Shall we all go together?' I suggested.

Before we got outside an uninvited guest had attached himself to us: Reginald Chatterton, the well-known glossy magazine writer and judge of beauty contests. Some time ago I had slept with him in passing, and some hours ago Oscar had spiked him with acid. We couldn't disown him.

'You don't know what I've just waded through,' he told Oscar breathlessly, his plump face rosy with exertion and his safari suit flapping. 'It's a nightmare. You must take me out of all this.' He paused. 'Do I sound paranoid?' He looked around at the four of us, and started to recognise me.

'It's you, isn't it?' he asked. I wondered how distorted I appeared. 'Have you heard what Oscar's done to me?'

'It's just what you needed, Reginald,' I told him. 'Are you having a nice time?'

'I don't know, am I supposed to, yes, I suppose I am, but it's time to leave. I've got a leader to write by tomorrow morning.'

'It should be worth reading,' Oscar said. 'We're going to eat, though I don't expect you're hungry.'

'Don't leave me here… I might freak out …' he laughed heartily, 'isn't that the expression?'

'You'd better come along with us, then,' said Oscar, 'you don't mind, do you?' he asked me. I pulled a face and shrugged.

In the car Reginald kept pointing at the night lights. 'Look,' he said, 'cheap neon light, garish, plastic imitations of the real thing… I expected something more profound …'

'I think the city lights are pretty,' said Alice, 'perhaps you want a light show.'

'You mean whirls and blobs and strobes?' he asked. 'You're not laughing at me, are you?'

I was sitting squashed between Oscar and Reginald. Oscar was fondling my knee with one hand and had the other inside my T-shirt, exploring my right tit. Reginald kept grasping for my free hand.

'You'll look after me, won't you, Tiptree,' and he suddenly thrust his sweaty face close to mine. 'You're an expert in these matters. Is it really like this?'

'Don't worry,' I told him.

All things considered, we ended up eating shepherds pie in The Windmill with Reginald fidgeting on his wooden chair.

'It's so bright… it's so plastic, it's a cheapo… I thought candles and joss sticks were the ticket …'

'In a minute, in a minute, we'll give you candles, joss sticks, sounds, everything in the text book,' Atmos told him. 'And even a downer to keep you quiet.'

Reginald's beady eyes flashed in paranoia.

'Do you think I need one?'

'It might soothe you a bit,' I told him.

Back in Mandrax Mansions we made Reginald lie between the speakers and listen to *Forever Changes*. I found myself sitting between Atmos and Oscar, who started running his hand up my leg. I shut my eyes and relaxed.

Suddenly I was aware of another hand stroking the back of my neck and I looked up to see Atmos touching me possessively. I looked towards Alice, who was smiling within a stoned security. My body had frozen between the two caressing hands. Atmos leant over and whispered in my ear.

'You're so suspicious. I can feel you tense when I touch you.'

'That's your fault,' I said coldly. 'You're intruding.'

'You know better than that,' he said gently. 'It was only a touch.'

Oscar shifted uneasily beside me. Alice was gazing dreamily at him and Reginald was watching us all suspiciously.

'Are you talking about me?' he called, and looked as though he was going to come over.

'Not at all, old man, lie back and enjoy the music,' Atmos told him.

'I need a cuddle,' he said plaintively. 'Tiptree, come over here and cuddle me.'

I turned to Oscar helplessly.

'I'll talk to him,' he said, and got up.

Atmos produced two white pills and told me to take them.

'I don't need downers,' I said.

'As your doctor, Miss Gibbon, I insist,' joked Atmos, putting his hand on my knee. He saw me looking at it.

'Now don't get uptight,' he said warningly.

'I'm not uptight,' I said aggressively. 'I just wish you could be more *platonic*, somehow.'

'I only touch you because I love you.'

Alice came over and sat in front of us. Atmos started touching her as well. She leant towards me.

'I really fancy Oscar,' she said suddenly. 'I'd really like to fuck him.'

'I don't want you to,' I heard myself say. 'I mean, *I* haven't had him yet.'

'I'm sorry,' she whispered, and put her arms round my neck, 'I didn't mean to freak you. I don't know why I said that.' And she plunged into some muddle all of her own.

I felt surrounded by confusion and picked up the pills. I went and knelt behind Oscar and put my arms round his waist.

'What's going on over there?' he demanded. 'Why don't we go back to my place?'

'That's a good idea,' I said. 'What about him?'

Reginald was talking to himself about tomorrow's leader.

'We'll drop him off. Bedtime, Reginald,' Oscar commanded. Reginald looked startled.

'I don't want to go home,' he said, 'I don't want to be alone. Will you stay with me tonight, Tiptree?' And he grabbed my hand.

'Let's get you home first,' said Oscar tactfully.

We left Atmos and Alice looking like a couple a thwarted cannibals on the cushions. Reginald didn't really want to go through his front door, he was full of excuses, and finally I offered him the downers. He looked at them suspiciously.

'Are they spiked?' he asked, holding them up to the light.

'They're sleeping pills,' Oscar said impatiently. 'Take them and go to bed and tomorrow you'll be fine.'

'I'll never get my leader written,' Reginald complained, reluctantly opening his front door. 'I think it's awfully mean of you to leave me like this. I'm still seeing things, you know.' He looked at us accusingly, but we'd already turned away. We looked back to see his solitary figure outlined in the doorway. I felt guilty and relieved both at once.

In the taxi we sat silent for a few minutes to recover. Then we got into this long intense stare that got closer and closer until it went out of focus and become a kiss that everything went into and I gave up watching what was happening and joined in. It was an amazing kiss that took me right into it until I was all tongue and lips and oral sensation. It was the kind of kiss that should have fallen backwards onto a bed and become a fuck but there was nowhere to fall, so we kissed and squirmed in the back of that taxi until we reached Oscar's basement.

The excitement of the kissing should have made Oscar sweep me straight into bed, but standing upright in his own environment seemed to put him in another dimension. He became very business-like, taking my coat, putting on a record, turning up the heat, flipping through some papers and managing to get in a couple of terse telephone calls before he disappeared into the kitchen. I was surrounded by shelves stuffed with books and magazines, tables covered with letters and articles and papers scattered everywhere like confetti. I sat on the saggy double bed amongst a vast selection of newsprint, from *Screw*, *The Realist*, *Liberation*, *The Voice*, to *The Spectator* and *The New Statesman*. Oscar reappeared with two cups of Ovaltine and sat at his desk, unable to keep his eyes off the scattered print. He picked up a sheaf of papers and sipped his Ovaltine. I tried to read a copy of *Good Karma*, but the print was dancing. I went and took the letters out of Oscar's hand.

'You love your work, don't you?' I asked, looking through the letters.

'Very boring really. Just readers' letters.'

'Well, read them some other time.'

We went and cleared ourselves a space on the bed.

'Look, I haven't even opened this morning's mail,' Oscar told me, reluctantly pushing aside a pile of envelopes.

Then he turned to me ardently. 'Let's have another of those kisses.' he said, and this time there was a bed underneath us. Our heads hit the newsprint and it started happening so fast we didn't have time to take our clothes off. The newspapers crackled under our bodies and the thing that pleased me most of all was to be fucking on top of *The New Statesman*. Oscar turned into a typewriter and filled me full of ink.

'Well,' said Oscar breathlessly, 'that all happened very fast. Incredible. That was really incredible.'

He started pulling my clothes off and running his hands critically over my body.

'Fantastic body, you're almost a boy.'

'Is that bad?' I asked.

'No, I like girls lean and athletic in bed.'

'Well, my father's an international footballer, if that's any help.'

'Yes, I read about that in the papers. I'm probably not the kind of guy you're used to going out with now you're so successful.'

'You never asked me out before,' I remarked.

'But I yearned for you, standing behind that cash register, so small and business-like. But you only had eyes for those skinny rock n'roll stars.'

Then he leapt up and fetched a chest expander from the corner, the kind you have to pump in and out, and with a fixed glaze of concentration in his eyes he pumped it twenty times. He did it every night before he went to bed, standing naked in his socks, as skinny and hairless as any pop musician.

We lay in bed listening to an aggressive American rock band shouting hate politics through the headphones while he kept time on my leg. Gradually the beat became more insistent and our bodies responded in time with the music. I had to hold my headphones to my head with one hand to stop them falling into my face and with the other try to untangle the flex that coiled itself relentlessly round our arms and legs.

I half opened my eyes to see Oscar raised on his arms chugging in and out of me like a bomber pilot. My excitement bordered on hilarity, especially when the flex threatened to castrate him, yet our movements seemed to fit like clockwork and his chest expander certainly kept him in vigorous condition. He was the best experience I had had in bed for a long time, for the majority of rock musicians had flogged their sexual fantasies to death on stage and in comparison were pretty limp between the sheets.

5

I was getting rather resentful at the way a lot of people assumed that Jay and I were married. When I told them we hadn't even slept together they looked disappointed because they thought I slept with everybody.

'We could marry just for tax reasons if you like, and the publicity would sell a few books,' Jay suggested.

'It wouldn't do much for my love life,' I said.

'I'm sure Oscar wouldn't mind – he understands a good hoax.'

'But *I'd* mind.'

My friendship with Atmos had been intended as an antidote to Jay being my sole confidant. Oscar was the antidote to the antidote. I spent a lot of time in his flat playing wife and doing all those domestic things that wasted Oscar's time when there was a revolution to look for. It was an amusing contrast to worry about the cooking instead of my identity. However, my identity continued to be topical and when Oscar's book on counterculture came out he found himself taken quite seriously and besieged by press and television.

Sometimes we were on the same programmes, and travelled together in a double first-class sleeper up to Scotland to do a religious programme. It was like being inside an adjustable chrome box with lots of buttons and dials for lighting and heat. Oscar immediately made himself at home, lying on his narrow bed and emptying thousands of papers out of his briefcase.

'I've just got to read a couple of articles,' he told me.

Everywhere I looked I could see images of me and Oscar in the mirrors.

'I'm bored,' I said. He handed me a book about the Chicago Conspiracy Trial to read.

'If you're interested,' he said, 'or not too stoned.'

I took the book silently, and tried to get a downer out of its bottle without him noticing the familiar rattle. But the lid wouldn't unscrew, and finally he noticed my fidgeting.

'Can you do this for me?' I asked.

'You take too many pills,' he said severely, but it didn't matter once I was floating and fuzzy. I had almost fallen asleep on page three when Oscar told me it was time for bed.

'I've never fucked on a train before,' he said, 'so let's try, shall we?'

The bed reminded me of hospital cubicles it was so hard and narrow, and we manoeuvred ourselves into the only possible position. At first I felt silly, but then I started to notice that as well as our own rhythm there was the rhythm of the train. Soon I wasn't sure which was our rhythm and which was the train. We entered a third rhythm that was a combination of the two and made us feel weightless. It was possible to be extremely energetic with very little effort, and the pleasure was extremely high. Oscar was most impressed, and told people for weeks afterwards what an incredible fuck he'd had with me on a train. He was becoming quite controversial and famous and it stirred my imagination.

'It's a literary romance,' I told Alice. 'What do you know about Saggitarians?'

'They fuck everybody,' she replied. 'They're as bad as Scorpios.'

I asked Oscar about this.

'I haven't had much chance lately,' he stared at me thoughtfully. 'There are several young ladies feeling rather neglected whom I should attend to some time, don't you think?'

I knew what I was supposed to think, but I couldn't say it.

'*I* like being with you,' I said sulkily.

'But think of all those pop musicians you're missing,' he said, 'or are you slipping down to the Speakeasy without telling me?'

'Sometimes,' I said. 'Why don't you come?'

'I'm no good in places like that,' he said. 'I'd rather read a book.'

'Are you an intellectual?' I asked.

'Yes,' he said emphatically.

Sometimes, when the present became too complicated, I would slip back into the past with a couple of downers and go rock-star prowling. I tried to turn it into a new game from a different angle, but mostly I just reassured myself it was an old movie that had lost its point.

'I can tell when you've been unfaithful,' Oscar would say. 'You have a delicious aura of half-guilt about you.'

Then he'd want to know who it was and what we did, but I felt embarrassed telling him because he wasn't Jay, and I found it difficult to be so open with someone I was sleeping with. I enjoyed Oscar in bed because he made me laugh. Yet I couldn't quite decide whether he was funny or not because of the way he pretended to take himself seriously, always hiding behind his deadpan stare. Half-way through a fuck he suddenly stopped dead and turned it on me. Then he started to twitch. The twitching gradually became a long convulsion, with Oscar gasping for breath and flailing my body with his arms. Just as suddenly he stopped completely still, and lay staring at me again.

'I'm sorry,' he whispered, 'this sometimes happens, I thought I told you about it ...' and his voice trailed away as he started twitching again. Between convulsions he managed to tell me he had these fits, but each time another attack would prevent him from explaining properly. I couldn't think of anything to do except watch with the occasional nervous giggle.

'What are you thinking?' he asked suddenly.

'Are you normal again?' I asked.

'What do you mean?'

'I mean those fits you were having ...'

'Tell me what you thought of them. Did they scare you?'

'Occasionally.'

'They were pretty real, weren't they?'

'I couldn't believe my eyes,' I told him. 'I didn't know what to think.'

He smiled, nodded, and finished fucking me. We fell asleep immediately.

I woke up first the next morning and started hunting round the bed for my sleeping rag. I had to push Oscar on to his back before I located it under his body, looking like a small squashed rat. Pressing it to my face, I stared at him defiantly as he complained.

'I wish you wouldn't bring that thing into my bed,' he grumbled, and reached out to put the phone back on the hook. It immediately started ringing, and he picked it up again. Through my early morning trance I listened to the problems, meetings, and arrangements that he had to cope with for the day.

'What about my breakfast, then?' he asked between phone calls. 'And the post,' he called, as I stumbled into the kitchen. I gathered the scattered envelopes and newspapers from the floor and threw them on to the bed. When I returned with toast and honey and a murky cup of tea, he'd sorted through it, and I climbed back between the sheets to read the morning's delivery of the psychedelic press. Oscar made a few more staccato phone calls then leapt out of bed for his shower. I could hear him singing about the Wombat and the Kangaroo under the hosepipe he'd rigged up over the bath. My reading was interrupted by busy people needing to speak to Oscar immediately, but I refused to do more than take down messages in his *Economist* diary.

Oscar returned wet and lively and full of natural speed.

'Still in bed?' he demanded. 'You sleep more than any chick I know.'

'Reading that freak argot is pretty exhausting,' I waved the *Cosmic Chronicle* at him, 'especially when you have to peer through coloured splodges to see the print. It almost makes it unreadable.'

He looked at me sternly.

'What shall I wear today?' he asked, pulling on his socks.

'Your green crushed trousers, your mauve T-shirt and your television cardigan, I suppose.'

'What's my television cardigan?'

'That patterned crochet thing you always wear on the box.'

'Do you like it? It was knitted in loving memory.'

'I'd like it if you didn't wear it so much.'

'I haven't got any clothes,' Oscar wailed. 'Why don't you do some shopping for me?' he suggested. 'I also need some things for the cottage.'

Oscar had just found an isolated country cottage that he intended to use as a retreat from London. We had spent an idyllic weekend battling with the elements and trying to get it organised. I got absorbed in painting the bathroom on acid with my hands numb from the freezing cold. His sister's Mini got stuck in the mud, and we floundered knee-deep for hours trying to move it. The nearest farm was half-an-hour away, and I got lost in the fields looking for a man in a tractor. We had to fuck a lot to keep ourselves warm in bed, for the only heated room was the kitchen, where I had to learn a whole new set of rules for cooking on an Aga. It was my first taste of country life since my childhood, and I liked being so far away from everything. We listened to country night noises and sat in front of an open fire.

'I feel like I've been married to you for thirty years,' Oscar suddenly said, and I wondered if he was being sentimental. He never spoke about the past or the future; he was too busy dealing with the present.

'It's nice being just you and me and no telephone,' I said.

'I'm trying to decide whether to put one in or not,' he said.

'You know what'll happen,' I told him.

'I'll keep the number extremely private,' he insisted. 'Just for emergencies. Now, how about some Fosters and some sex in front of this romantic fire?'

6

The interest in the book had escalated into movie deals. Mason was trying to set up a package deal with himself as a producer and liked having me along to tell them what it was all about. I sat in exclusive clubs and restaurants burbling my stoned nonsense and hardly able to eat a thing.

'You shouldn't get so stoned, sweetheart,' Mason told me. 'They can't understand what you're talking about.'

'Well, find someone who can. *That's the kind of person who should be making the movie.* Anyway, I like to be high. Don't you?'

'Sure I do,' he agreed.

'What do you take, then?' I asked.

'I get high on reality,' he said, and seemed to mean it.

'What's that?' I giggled.

'Why don't you try some other way.' Mason suggested. 'I meditate.'

'How do you do that?' I asked.

'A friend of mine makes records of things like meditation, astrology, yoga, black magic. I use him as my spiritual advisor. Are you interested?'

'Yes.'

'I'll introduce you to him, but first try listening to the meditation record. And don't take any drugs beforehand.'

'Better do it first thing in the morning,' I said, 'I'm too far gone today.'

He turned his shades on me.

'No more before dinner,' he said. 'Sandy Irving is bringing along a young American director who wants to meet you.'

'It's time I pulled a movie director,' I said.

Cy Henry could be the first, I thought, as I sized him up across the dinner table.

'Could you blow the candle out?' I asked him. 'It's flickering too much.'

I ordered an artichoke to keep me busy for the whole meal.

'Is that all you're having?' Cy asked me.

'Meat makes me think too much,' I said. 'I like your Chairman Mao badge.'

He fingered it proudly on the collar of his non-look denim jacket.

'Don't give me any bullshit about Hitler and Napoleon,' he said, 'this cat could run circles round them.'

'Is he so clever?'

'He's given those people a direction, something to believe in.'

'Hitler tried that.'

'Bah! He was fucked up. I tell you, Mao's Commies will be the ones who come out of all this on top.'

'My parents think the West is declining like the fall of the Roman Empire and that everything is a Communist plot.'

'Mao doesn't need to plot when there are cocksuckers like Nixon around. America is on the verge of revolution and anarchy and I know whose side I'm on. What do you think?'

'Very little about politics. Most of my friends believe in the revolution.'

'What revolution?'

'The one that will change everything.'

'Nixon is the revolution.'

'Does he know?'

'Depends how clever he is. Either that, or he's very stupid.'

'If you like.'

I wished I could argue like Oscar.

'So tell me about being a groupie,' Cy said. 'I know a few myself,' and he reeled off some real star-fucker names.

'I'm nothing as grand as that,' I apologised.

'Yes you are,' he said. 'You've written a book.'

I explained everything and he understood. Not only that, he enjoyed it and re-interpreted it visually as I went along, stimulating my capacity to exaggerate and emphasise little details that both of us understood were important to a film. By the end of the meal we still had more to say, but Mason and Sandy Irving seemed to have run out of gossip and negotiations and couldn't pick up on our conversation.

Cy and I split to some film-writer's pad where there was an orgy going on. We were invited to join in, but managed to find a secluded sofa away from all the action. We exchanged stories until it was time to get more personal, and then Cy started getting down to some heavy petting. Squashed together full-length on the sofa, struggling against each other through our clothing, I found it all very uncomfortable and childish. It was starting to get light outside and I felt like being in bed where we could either do things properly or go to sleep. It took some hinting; Cy was probably trying to get it over and done with on the sofa. It was the beginning of another day when we finally straggled off to the spare room he occupied in a film friend's house.

'Got a lot of velvet suits,' I observed.

'I haven't got *any*,' he said. 'They're all past it.'

Cy was a well-preserved forty with a wardrobe like a King's Road groover. He showed me a chamois leather T-shirt and two-toned boots he'd just bought. He was also very impressed by a pair of leather trousers he'd had made specially.

'They must get sweaty in the summer,' I said.

'Not in this country,' he retorted. 'Here, feel how soft they are.'

When he took his clothes off he looked like something known as a 'real man'. Younger generation freaks were pale and skinny, but Cy had a Hollywood sun-tan on a muscleman frame.

'Have you pulled a lot of movie stars?' I asked him.

'Quite a few.'

'I bet they like your body.'

'I have to watch my waistline,' he pulled his diaphragm in and patted his stomach.

I took my clothes off neatly in a corner so I wouldn't leave anything behind and got into bed. He looked at me lying beneath the sheets and drew the curtains on the early morning before taking his trousers off.

'Let's get down to that reputation of yours,' he said, and then we were back where we'd left off except there was a lot more flesh around. I thought I had a lot of energy in bed but Cy certainly pipped my post. I had been bent double on my back so long I could hardly move my position. My responses to Cy's plunges had become faint and mechanical.

'My ovaries ache,' I whispered.

'Do something to me for a while,' he said, and lay invitingly on his back. I knew what he was checking on. I slid my tongue slowly down his stomach and traced it round and down between his legs. Then I softly covered him with my mouth and let my lips slide lightly up and down, stroking him gently with my spare fingers. I increased the speed and pressure for a few seconds then I stopped and looked up at him. He was watching me.

'Like to tease, do you?' He took my head between his hands and forced it down again. I widened my eyes in shock, only to blink violently when the Anglepoise flashed on. I tensed and squinted up at Cy.

'Pretend you're in the movies,' he said, adjusting it straight at my face. I tried. 'Smile,' he instructed, 'you gotta look like you're enjoying it.'

I bared my teeth at him menacingly and pressed them lightly into the thin skin.

'You wouldn't,' he said.

I tried all my tricks but couldn't break his control. I don't think he was really there, he was muttering to himself and fidgeting with the Anglepoise, changing the lighting angles and even strobing me. Inwardly annoyed, and outwardly exhausted, I stopped with tears in my eyes from the effort and glare. He wiped them away gently.

'Did you like it so much?' he cooed. 'Now I've got a treat for you. Turn over.'

I stared at him without seeing. I couldn't tell him. Slowly I slid down on my stomach and spread my legs. As he penetrated me from behind I shot forward and gripped the sides of the bed to stop myself falling on to the floor. I gritted my teeth and blacked out my mind to take the pain. It had to happen, and it had to be my secret. The pain dissolved into a numb kind of pleasure. It was quite puzzling, because I couldn't feel anything until he took it out. It was after eight in the morning and he still hadn't finished. I fell asleep while he came into me again, and dreamed he was my father. I became inter-changeable with my mother and saw myself wearing rollers.

I woke in the afternoon, still struggling with my parents. I found Cy sitting on a pouffe in the adjoining room with cards spread out in front of him on a low table. He didn't look anything like my father but kept making me think of him.

'Let me show you some tricks,' he said, and pulled a card out from between my legs.

'That's a party trick,' he said. 'You look too dopey to cope with anything more complicated.'

When I came back from the bathroom he was engrossed in a chess game with himself. He sipped at a bowl of soup in between moves. I chewed a piece of gum and watched him for a while.

'So I'm off,' I announced.

'I'm leaving too, so hang on,' and he froze the chess board in his mind for a moment before standing up. He was all in leather today and creaked. He picked up a large plastic bag.

'Walk across the park, put my washing in, then down the King's Road to see what's happening in the Casserole. What about you?'

'Taxi home to meditate. Mason says it'll make me very high.'

'"He who speaks does not know, he who knows does not speak,"' Cy quoted. 'Do you like that?'

'That's clever.'

'I've got just the thing for you,' he said, and fetched me a book of Chinese riddles.

'Call me when you've read it,' he said, and wrote his phone number on the back.

7

I lay in the bath telling Alice about Cy while she sat on the bidet fingering her snatch.

'I'm down,' Alice said. 'I've cried twice today. I did an audition for a margarine commercial, they were looking for Queen Guinevere. You know this feeling I have about being re-incarnated, well, I was just vibing those guys, knowing they had to choose me. I went as I am because that's how I see myself, but they just didn't see, you know, they just didn't see.'

'What did they see?'

'Oh, they were looking for their own plastic concept, and couldn't recognise the real thing. They saw an untidy flat-chested freak on a crazy trip, I guess.'

She stood up and dried herself.

'I'm going to walk in the park and look at the flowers,' she announced.

'I'm going to meditate,' I told her.

'Maybe I'll do that instead,' she hesitated.

'Let me try it alone first,' I said, 'you'll make me giggle.'

'I suppose so,' she said.

Atmos was at his Family Planning Clinic, so the flat was clear. I arranged the cushions, half drew the curtains, lit joss-sticks and candles, put the record on and dashed to sit down before it started. I had to re-play the breathing instructions several times before I could get it right. I kept forgetting how to breathe while concentrating on the subsequent instructions. I had to stop the record again to fetch a flower to stare into. I lost myself in it wondering how Mason coped with this part. I missed two sets of images and found myself on the Ladder of Light, so I had to start again to make the correct transitions. I had reached the top of the Ladder of Light and was about to merge with the sun when the ring of the telephone shattered into my mind. I picked up the receiver so fast to shut off the intrusion that I hadn't properly reconnected my brain.

'Every day the deal is where it was yesterday, which is where it was the day before that, and not very different to where it's been for weeks,' Jay's voice barked over the telephone. 'And I want to know what's being done about it.'

'Ask Mason,' I said faintly, trying to think.

'You ask him. You're the one he takes to all those meetings.'

'They're all a lot of nonsense to me.'

'Well, you'd better start understanding film deals if you don't want to be sold up the river. Anyway, why do you sound so far away? Where are you? And what happened last night with that movie director you had to meet?'

'I'm listening to the Voice of the Inner Glow and can't possibly speak now. I'm trying to meditate.'

'Is that Mason's idea? He's trying to take control of your mind, you know. He knows you're hung up on him.'

'I'm not hung up on him, it's just a father complex I've got. I had one last night as well.'

'Have you written it down in your diary?'

'I haven't had time yet. I'm trying to meditate while the flat's empty... I must get on with it now.'

'Meditation and all that Chinese bullshit will turn you into a vegetable,' he said.

'The vegetable is at peace,' I told him pompously. I could feel him disapproving in the pause.

'I'll check with you later,' he said, and hung up.

I felt annoyed at Jay's non-synchronisity, and had a smoke.

Then I started the record on the second track and turned into the Tree of Life. I spread upwards to the end of a tingling leaf, then outwards to become all the leaves in the forest, all the trees, the whole forest, which spread all over the world. And the world became infinity…

When I came down I felt quite faint and extremely stoned. I tried to gather my concentration for the River of Delights, but the Tree of Life had taken all my energy and I couldn't apply myself to changing from a water lily into a kingfisher. I was on my third attempt when the front door banged and Alice blew into the room.

'I've just had this amazing adventure in the park,' she was high and breathless, 'this flash sports car started cruising me so I looked at the driver. He looked like an affluent groover and asked me if I was an actress. I said sometimes and he said he was sure he'd seen me in something. This and that, I said, I haven't found the right part yet. Then he handed me a card and asked me if I'd come and test for him. I couldn't believe it, it was like the movies, but I took the card and promised to get in touch. Then he said how about lunch tomorrow and I said that's rather early, so he said all right, dinner. Then I got confused and gave him my phone number… does he just want a fuck or do you think he'll make me a star?'

'Was he real?' I asked, 'or had you been sniffing the flowers again?'

'Yes, maybe he was just another hallucination… but the card's real and it says Harvey Legrand, London, Hollywood, Rome …' She brightened. 'All kinds of strange things happen to me in the park. It's another world… you should walk in the park, Tiptree.'

'Not until I've got my own,' I said, 'without any people in it.'

'I love the people,' Alice said. 'I freak them out by dancing like a wood nymph around the trees. They don't know what's happening, man.'

'What are you going to do about the movie man?' I asked.

'I'm going to throw a Ching,' she said, 'I could do with one anyway, things have changed since the Moon went into Leo.'

Atmos came in later with news of the super-hype. To launch a new group two young hustlers were flying a plane-load of celebrities and media-men across the Atlantic on credit to see Bermuda Schlitz open at the Fillmore East and the performance would be turned into a film.

'I'm to be the magic vibe dispenser for when people run low on energy,' Atmos patted his black box, 'and you can be my lovely lady assistant,' he told Alice.

'My Ching said I would cross the great water,' she said, 'and not eating at home brings good fortune, so let's got to the Baghdad House.'

There was a lot of status-squabbling over the air tickets amongst the straights and alternatives. Oscar wouldn't let me take any dope with me, so on the morning I got up especially early and smoked it all. I dizzily watched Oscar squeezing as many possible copies of his book into a brief-case already full of papers.

'Can you fit any into your basket?' he asked. 'I've got a lot of people over there I want to lay books on. I hope you're not getting stoned and inefficient.'

After going to the wrong terminal, then sitting through a four-hour delay, and an emergency landing on the way, we were hooted through the traffic by limousines to arrive just in time. Oscar was dashing around talking to people he'd arranged to meet so I sat with Alice and Atmos and listened to the music.

'Lead guitarist too fat, singer too pretty, drummer too mangy, so it would have to be the organist,' I whispered to her.

'Oh, I think the singer has personality vibes,' she said. 'I get off on him.'

'No, he's too sure of himself. The organist looks insecure and moody. I bet he writes the music.'

When the main American group came on to play Oscar had found a seat beside me and was fiddling with the off-duty tape recorder he'd managed to score during the emergency landing. Seeing all those American rock musicians made me think of Larry and wonder who he was playing with and whether I'd every see him again. My sentimental reveries were interrupted by Oscar wanting me to help him with his machine, and suddenly I resented him. I resented Atmos too, who had taken a lot of speed and was talking incredulously about everything in sight. I resented Jay who kept talking about our book and the publicity tour we would be giving around America. I resented Alice and her astral innocence, and I resented the fact that I wouldn't have time to find Larry. This was the closest I'd got to him for two years and by tomorrow night I'd be gone. I resolved to find him when we returned next month, I wouldn't leave without finding him and finding out what all this meant. Larry was back in my head, and no one else mattered.

8

I had my first row with Oscar later that night. Oscar said he might not have time for sleep during this American Experience, though we were obliged to register at the hotel provided by the hype. He told me to get a double room while he made some telephone calls, which I found harder than I expected. I found I had been paired with Jay on some list, and getting things changed would be complicated.

'Don't let some bureaucratic list defeat you,' Oscar instructed me, 'go and sort it out.'

I was tired and didn't care where my room was as long as I could crash for a few hours. But Oscar had other plans, and bustled me off to Max's Kansas City where the best freaks in town go.

'This is one of the ten best people in New York,' I was introduced to Marty Soper, a sorrowful-looking degenerate.

'Are you famous?' He had a cynical drawl.

'Slightly. Are you?'

'Sure, everybody's famous here, there's nothing else left to do.'

'How's your love life?' I heard someone ask Oscar from the other end of the table.

'Sitting opposite me,' he replied, grinning, but I could only stare across at him blankly. I turned back to Marty and told him I was coming back next month and could I get in touch with him so that he could turn me on to some interesting people. He seemed willing to help and I wanted to sleep with him.

'Hi!' he said to some passing friends, 'I'm with some English celebrities,' and he put his arm round me and smiled like he was posing for a photo. There were lots of freaks milling round the tables and an exotic dark chick came and draped herself over Marty while he laughed at her gently with his sad brown eyes.

'That's Cornelius Belvedere,' Marty told me, 'only he's known as the Venus Fly Trap. He's just starred in a movie about himself as a chick so he'll never have to be ashamed again. You'd like him.' Marty leant against me lazily.

'I like too many people,' I said, 'I haven't got time to like any more.'

Marty had half risen in his chair to identify a new entrance.

'Look who I see!' he said, and stood up. 'I'm just going to throw a drink of something at the Moon Goddess. I'll be back,' he added, and wove his way laconically through the people to a tall blonde Warhol queen, who patted him on the head like a spaniel.

Marty was with us when we got into my first yellow cab to take us to my first New York apartment that was all shelved sections within a minute area. We all squashed in and smoked grass through flavoured skins.

'Whose place is this?' Marty asked me, looking round doubtfully.

I pointed out the middle-aged veteran of bohemia that Oscar had insisted on taking us all to see. His plump lady wife was squeezing in and out with cups of tea. I could feel Oscar's eye on me as I deliberately positioned myself with Marty to watch some late-night movie on the twenty-four-hour tube. I could get no positive reaction out of Marty but felt inhibited by Oscar's presence. When Oscar wanted to leave I wanted to stay. We had an impatient row in the doll-size kitchen and Oscar left. I couldn't make it on my own so I followed and we insulted each other on the street. I sulked and went straight to sleep in my separate bed. A few hours later I was woken by the central heating to find Oscar already off on his massive time-table. I was relieved to miss a guided tour of the revolution and spent the day with Jay being tourists. We weren't in any hurry because we knew we'd be back.

Returning to the hotel to meet up with everyone we were in time to catch the end of the Bermuda Schlitz press reception, and I got to look at the group close up. I was right about the organist and decided to play my role out. Amongst other vultures I looked down on the instant groupies hovering round our super-stars of the future. It was easy to get invited up to their suite for a smoke, for they were impressed and giggled when they found out who I was.

We had to split up to be driven to the plane, and some freaks who had got too stoned decided to try their luck and stay behind. Strapped into a seat between Oscar and Jay I located the group sitting in the first class section, surrounded by their managerial unit. When the safety lights were out everyone started swirling around the aircraft. The straights started drinking beer and the heads gathered in little groups to smoke grass in the freedom of international air space. A number of Fleet Street men complained that the grass fumes were sending them to sleep and preventing them from finishing their copy. There were also complaints about the porn papers that Oscar had smuggled on board and was busy distributing. Revitalised by an argument on the way back to his seat, Oscar turned his tape machine up full volume and started smoking.

'I hope you've recovered from last night,' Oscar said. 'Had our first row,' he leaned across me to inform Jay.

'Oscar got too bossy,' I explained.

'You were being so feeble... she was trying to pull a well-known homosexual,' he informed Jay. 'I wasn't behaving any differently from usual, was I?' he demanded.

'No, just twice as much.'

'I just didn't have time to cope with a hysterical female.'

'I know, all those people to see and facts to exchange. Why didn't you stay in America where there's a real revolution?'

'There's a lot to be done in Europe,' he told me sternly.

I left Jay to listen to the European situation because I had seen a vacant seat beside the organist.

'Did you dream of this?' I asked him.

'Oh yes, it's one of those fantasies, isn't it?' he said.

'What were you doing before you were discovered?'

'Living on two bob a day and waiting for something to happen. Though I never really expected all this.'

'Who's paying for it?'

'We are, I suppose. Our managers are fixing up lots of deals. We just take a small wage at the moment to keep us going.'

'No holidays on the Riviera?'

'Oh no, the holiday's over, we're hoping for a lot of work from all the publicity.'

'Did it get you a lot of groupies?' I asked him.

'I was too freaked out by everything else to notice,' he apologised, 'I think Stan pulled something, but the other two are married, you know.'

'Didn't groupies come into your fantasy, then?'

'Not yet,' he said.

'It would be nice to start with something special, wouldn't it?'

'I've just lost one of those,' he said, 'by being too nice.'

'You won't have to be nice any more,' I told him. 'You're the desirable object now.'

'Is it really like that?' he asked. 'How confusing.'

'It's not so bad… is it?' And I leant forward and kissed him. I could feel the shock run through him and pulled back before he could respond.

'What do you mean?' he asked.

'I mean I've come to pull you because you're a rock n'roll star and that's my trade.'

'I thought you'd just come to talk to me,' he protested.

'I might do that as well.'

'You won't find me very interesting, I'm afraid.'

'That doesn't matter. You're part of the great plot.'

'What's that?'

'I was sent on this plane trip to pull you, I mean, it's so obvious isn't it? Doesn't it all fit in with the fantasy you've found yourself in?'

'Definitely,' he said, and wanted me to kiss him again.

'Too much,' he said before our faces met, 'too much!'

Everybody could see me doing my number, but I couldn't bear to read their thoughts. After I had got young Billy thoroughly worked up I told him I had to go back to my friends.

'I've got a few things to sort out,' I told him.

'You are coming back?' he asked anxiously.

'I'd like to sit with you for the touch-down,' I told him, 'if there's room.'

'Of course there's room,' he said, 'I'll fix it.'

I sat guiltily between Oscar and Jay and didn't know how to begin.

'Been somewhere?' asked Jay.

'Just talking to people,' I replied.

'Anyone in particular?' he asked.

It was easier to tell Jay and let Oscar overhear.

'There's this organist from the group ...' I paused, and nudged Jay with a grin.

'Going to show him what it's like to be a super-star?' asked Jay.

'I thought I'd give him a taste ...' I turned to Oscar, 'you don't mind, do you?'

'Why no, no, of course not,' he said emphatically.

'I knew you'd say that,' I told him. 'Oscar believes in freedom,' I said to Jay, 'it's so convenient.'

My face felt dry with exhaustion and wet with kisses when we emerged into the early Monday morning. Jay got out his Instamatic to catch me clinging to my pop star with Oscar scowling and the whole thing being filmed.

When Billy and I finally found ourselves with nobody to tell us what to do we hardly knew where to start.

'Where do you live?' I asked him, 'are you being kept in a nice hotel?'

'I'm afraid I'm still at my mum's,' he said.

So we went to Mandrax Mansions where Atmos was still rapping about the weekend and Alice lay watching me through her lashes and dreaming. By noon Billy and I were in the mattress on the floor and he was fucking me like he'd been on a severe diet. Then he told me about the chick he'd loved and how cruel she'd been, and I thought how good I'd be to Larry if he would love me like that.

'The more I gave her the less she wanted.'

I wanted Larry to give me everything so that I could give him everything in return.

'She played games with me ...'

Larry would stop me doing that, and I would let him.

'I only wanted to love her ...'

And I wanted Larry to love me so that I could lose myself in his identity and never have to think again. Oscar had certainly not allowed this and I wanted to explore a deeper involvement. I wanted to know there was one guy who was everything, perhaps like Alice felt about Atmos. Until then, I'd just keep playing.

'Is it a paradox?' he asked.

'Most of the time,' I said.

'Maybe I chose the wrong chick,' and he looked at me shyly.

I gave him four days in a darkened room before I got claustrophobia.

9

I couldn't feel the same about Oscar now and I didn't want to see him. Cy was busy on a mickey-mouse film, for Mason hadn't liked him, and was now looking in the direction of Hollywood. I was left to the mercy of Atmos and Alice but wouldn't give anything away. I wanted to confide in Jay about Larry because he knew it from the beginning, but felt I shouldn't have to.

It took a real freak to catch my fancy, something as bizarre as a politician, so that Mason could make jokes about Christine Keeler, who had turned up at one of his parties.

Called upon to give our version of the permissive society at a Young Conservatives' Forum I found myself talking to Ernest Peckwater, young Tory candidate for the safe seat of South Boddington.

'I didn't know they allowed politicians to be under 50,' I said.

'What do you know about politics?' he demanded.

'I'm looking for someone to teach me,' I said.

'I'll give you some lessons,' he said, 'what do you want to know?'

'I'd like another version of Vietnam and the Middle East,' I said. 'I'm trying to be objective.'

'That's not possible,' he said, 'when there's so much at stake.'

'Do you mean power?' I asked, 'I'm fascinated by power.'

He looked round cautiously, then lowered his voice.

'So am I,' he confided. 'All kinds.'

I thought he was pretty racy in his suit laying down the law about the permissive society and the dock strikes and hoped he didn't think my short speech on free love and VD to irrelevant. He reassured me that it was most entertaining and asked me out to dinner.

'I've never been out with a man in a real suit before,' I said.

'What do you mean, a real suit?'

'I mean the kind of suit my father would wear, I don't call velvet suits real suits, do you?'

'What on earth do you call them, then?'

'Just suits. And that's a real suit,' I pointed at his chalk-stripe straightjacket.

I wanted to show him to Atmos and Alice so made him stop off for a smoke on the way after I'd found out his attitude.

'Of course I smoke pot,' he said, 'though I'm not in favour of it.'

'What does that mean?' I asked.

'I'm against legislation. It would never do for the working class to get turned on.'

'I think it would be nice for them.'

'It's hard enough to get them to work as it is. Amphetamines are all they should be allowed.'

'That's mostly what they take,' I said. 'Does the National Health see to that?'

'Now you're getting the picture,' he said, 'and don't tell your friends who I am.'

Nobody could do much except stare at each other, so I took him off and waited until later to tell them. The food was boring and there was nobody to look at so I listened to Ernest's anecdotes about university life. He was the only one with a fridge for the champagne and a secretary to type his papers. He ate his way through the James Bond menus and must have irritated his friends, for they shut him in a laundry basket pretending to be SMERSH. By pudding he was talking about sex and after coffee he invited me back to his apartment.

His apartment made me think of men-only clubs and Queen Victoria. There were glass-fronted bookcases containing ancient leather volumes, and heavy couches and spindly tables with knick-knacks.

'I can only offer you a drink,' he said, 'I have to be discreet in my own premises, you know.'

I said I'd have a Kummel and looked for the sound system.

'I'd like some music,' I said, and he turned on a small radio. It sounded tinny and stupid.

'Thank you for the meal,' I said, 'though we didn't talk much politics.'

'You're not really interested in politics, are you?' he asked.

'Some of the time.'

'Well, now it's time for something else. What do you like to do in bed?'

'Haven't you read the book?' I asked.

'I want to hear you tell me.'

'How can I when I never know till afterwards?' I said.

He sighed.

'You're very hard to excite,' he said.

'You haven't even touched me yet.'

'I suppose you need to be whipped with an electric wire,' he said. 'Would you like that?'

'Not at all,' I said. 'Would you?'

'You're so cold. You don't respond.'

'What to?'

'My suggestions.'

'Try some others.'

'Maybe we should go into the bedroom,' he suggested.

I thought so too, and found myself in a practical

mahogany bedroom with Ernest turning some leather-bound photos to the wall.

'It's the lady I love,' he said, 'I couldn't bear her to see.'

'Nothing's happened yet.'

'I'm waiting for you.'

I took my clothes off and got into the large bed.

'Your turn,' I said, and he unbuttoned himself.

His body fell on my like a sack of dough and his cock was pretty soggy too. There wasn't much I could do with any of him if he didn't shift his weight.

'Can you kiss?' I asked, wondering why he didn't.

'It wouldn't be right,' he said, 'under the circumstances.'

'Do you mean her?' I waved at the walls. 'What does she do to you?'

'That's sacred,' he said, 'you must understand,' he pleaded, 'that's not what I want. I need something… different.'

'Perhaps you'd like to tie me up. Then you can do what you want.'

'Why didn't you say so before?'

He plopped down on me again, trying to stuff his non-erection up my unresponsive snatch. I couldn't lend a hand or open my legs properly but that was his problem. I wondered how long he'd be when he stopped.

'Is that it?' I asked.

He rolled off me.

'I'm sorry, I can't, no offence, it's always the same.'

'Her again?'

He got up and turned a photo round and stared at a middle-aged lady.

'She won't let me have any fun,' he said petulantly.

'Is that her?'

'This is my mother,' he said indignantly. 'And this is the Lady Elizabeth.' He turned round the wife of a well-known elder statesman.

'Isn't she beautiful?' he asked.

'And powerful too. Do you work for his Lordship?'

'What do you know about these kind of people?' he asked disdainfully. 'They're above you.'

'I sleep in a Lord's bedroom and you're a very bad fuck, that's what I know.'

I had had enough and couldn't stop. I harangued him while I got dressed and demanded to be taken home immediately. He cringed and apologised all the way home under my criticism of his abilities.

'I don't expect we'll be seeing each other again,' he said with dignity outside my door. 'So I'll say goodbye.'

'Good luck,' I said, and went inside to turn it into a joke for Atmos and Alice.

10

The Germans were very excited about their discovery of groupies and insisted on launching the book in style. Our presence would ensure the kind of publicity that couldn't fail to make it a success.

The night before I had to choose between an impotent revolutionary and an anxious film promoter. I must have been thinking out loud, for Rik Douglas the film promoter leant towards me and said emphatically:

'What are *you* into? Those are *heavy* vibes!'

So that got him the vote, and, anyway, the revolutionary had had his chance last week when I had spent a whole night trying to sort out his problem. When Rik Douglas told me I was a king-sized lady I knew he wouldn't last either, but I wanted an audience for my last night. I had to be up at seven the next morning to finish packing and make myself look crazy for television cameras that would be meeting us off the plane. But the phone had got knocked off the hook by movements in the night, so the first thing I knew was an insistent ringing at the front door. Jay stood there radiant in a three-dimensional rainbow shirt and starry trousers. He saw me bleary and tangled, and cursed. I pulled myself into an old lace dress and patchwork jacket and tied it all together with an art nouveau scarf. Rik sat in bed looking foolish while I threw anything I could think of into my tapestry hold-all.

'Oh the jet set,' he mocked, 'what it's like to be a star.'

'Who's he?' demanded Jay. 'Where did he come from?'

'I met him last night,' I explained.

Jay peered down at the mattress.

'Do I know you?' he asked.

Rik announced his name and held out his card but Jay didn't seem to notice.

'Are you responsible for all this?' Jay asked him, but didn't wait for an answer. 'Who's got the tickets?' he suddenly demanded.

'You're supposed to have them,' I said.

'So I am,' he said, 'well, don't forget your passport.'

'I'm ready,' I announced.

'You look like a laundry basket,' Jay said, 'but I supposed it'll have to do. Come on.'

'Goodbye then,' I called to Rik as Jay propelled me out of the door.

'I'll be getting to know you a lot better when you come back,' Rik said meaningfully, 'a *lot* better,' and he blew a kiss as the door slammed behind us.

When we touched down in Frankfurt an announcement was read out: 'Would Miss Gibbon come to the exit door, please, no one can leave the plane until Miss Gibbon comes to the exit door.' Jay propelled me between the people, and Wolfgang the Publisher was waiting to shake my hand in the hatchway. We all burst out into the daylight and stepped elegantly down the silver stair-trolley just like important people do on the News. There were two camera crews that preceded us across the tarmac. They made us walk through customs twice to get their shot right and I cursed myself for coming without any dope. Jay and I were shown into the back seat of a large car that had a man behind a camera facing us from the front seat. Two men kept thrusting microphones and questions at us.

'I must apologise,' I said, 'but I've only just got up and can't answer any questions before I've had a bath.'

They thought I was being funny and took no notice. I let

Jay cope, and got half-an-hour in the hotel to sort myself out before being filmed eating a traditional German meal in some remote inn.

'Eat up, eat up,' they encouraged me, 'have some cider.'

I was confronted by a great assortment of sausage meat, and shook my head.

'I can't eat meat for breakfast,' I said, and they all laughed heartily.

'Tell us what you think of our traditional German cider,' asked a man looking like a ski-instructor, and a boom mike swung into my face. I sipped suspiciously.

'It tastes like flat beer,' I said.

'Oh, don't say such things about our cider,' he chided, 'the people will be most upset.'

'Perhaps it's very potent?' I asked hopefully.

'I'm afraid not,' he laughed.

We were whirled round shops full of books and posters and shook a lot of hands and signed a lot of books until it was time to visit the offices of an underground magazine. The offices and the magazine were both pretty glossy, and I wondered who was paying. Recording an interview for the next issue the young reporter suddenly produced a press cutting that stated I did not intend to sleep with anyone while I was in Germany.

'Do you intend to keep your word?' he asked.

'Until I change my mind, I suppose.'

'It says here you have a weakness for underground writers. Well, you're surrounded by them. Is there anyone here you might fancy?'

'Him,' I pointed at the most likely looking hairy, 'I'll have him.' I went over to get a closer look.

'Can I have him now?' I asked.

Wolfgang stepped between us and took my arm.

'Come and have some tea first,' he said. 'Siegfried will be at the party later.'

'Try and score me some acid,' I managed to instruct the bewildered Siegfried.

'So, that reminds me,' said Wolfgang, 'I have a present for you.' And he led me out of range of the cameras.

'We know you don't like to be without so we managed to get you this.' He produced a two-ounce deal wrapped in tissue paper. 'I hope it will be enough.'

'Plenty,' I said, 'how very thoughtful.'

Back again in the hotel to prepare for the party, Jay and I tested it out.

'Is this German shit?' asked Jay, as it crumbled doubtfully between his fingers. I sniffed it.

'It certainly isn't Afghani,' I said.

After smoking furiously for half-an-hour and getting nowhere we decided it was camel's piss and boot polish. Grade X.

'It *is* German shit,' Jay said. 'Is this what turns them on over here?'

'I'm hoping for some acid later.'

'Diluted speed, if you're lucky. You look as though you could do with some.'

Siegfried had managed to get me one purple acid tab which did little more than make me edgy, but that was better than nothing. I bluffed my way through the exposure until I could split with Siegfried. Jay was being drooled over by a glamorous lady in corsets, whom he helplessly brought along with us. After a pizza, which was the only edible thing I could find in Germany, Jay's lady drove us back to our hotel in her small Beetle. We assumed that because we had double rooms there would be no objection to taking people in.

'Too late for visitors,' we were told sternly as we picked up our keys.

'That's nonsense,' Jay said, 'we have double rooms.'

'That's because we didn't have any singles left. You're booked as singles.'

We assumed this was some moral rule, and didn't realise that if we'd offered to pay the extra our visitors would have been welcome. It was too late to contact Wolfgang for advice, so we went and sat in the car. I was extremely annoyed at being thwarted, and refused to believe I couldn't get a man into my bedroom if I wanted to. Jay was already struggling with the corsets in the back when I told Siegfried to come with me. I took him round to the back of the hotel and insisted that he climb up to the third floor and get in through one of the windows, though I couldn't be sure which was mine.

'Otherwise I'll go in and throw you down some knotted sheets,' I said. 'What do you say?'

He thought it was all too risky and suggested we sit on a bench for a while. I wasn't really interested, so we kissed under a lamp-post for a few minutes before returning to the car. The windows were steamed up and it was rocking gently to the exertions inside. I opened the door impatiently to find Jay in the middle of being given a blow job.

'I'm going into the hotel,' I told him.

'Hang on a few minutes,' he said, 'and I'll come with you.'

So Siegfried and I kissed and exchanged useless promises to fill in the time it took for Jay to come.

I had a star tantrum in Munich and sulked in my Hilton-style suite. There were too many reporters and nothing to get high on, and I'd had an unsatisfactory night with neither Siegfried or my sleeping rag, which I had forgotten in the mattress along with Rik Douglas. Jay gave me a lecture and went off to try and score me some acid. Finding his way to the Schwabing District, he managed to strike a bargain in Oblomov's Tea Room. The two flat white pills looked so negative and anonymous that I expected even less reaction that the Frankfurt Purple. I swallowed both of them, and within half-an-hour was overcome with hilarity at having been deceived by appearances. I was alone for the initial rush so nobody knew how high I was by the time we were all ready to leave for the Crash Club and the Super-Groupie Competition.

As we stepped into the discotheque we were isolated in a pool of light that attempted to follow us to our reserved area. I ignored all the questions as out of turn until I was finally arranged in my seat at the ringside and the light could stop fluttering like a nervous yo-yo. Focusing through the glare I could see the dance floor filling up with spawning salmon armed with cameras and microphones. Being asked to look three different ways while answering four different questions and signing endless books at the same time I felt like a puppet on too many strings. While this was all going on in front of us there were important people crowding round our table introducing themselves to the backs of our heads. A Bavarian prince and his princess tried to sit down and talk to us but were told to wait their turn. They kept asking to be introduced, but nobody had time for that.

'Did you do the book for money and if so isn't that rather immoral?' asked a man with smelly breath who'd been trying to catch my attention for too long.

'I did it for fun,' I said, and turned to another flashlight.

'What's it like to be stared at all the time?' caught my attention from another direction and I studied my answer.

'I just pretend it's not me they're staring at, but someone who looks like me. I'm staring at them from somewhere else without them knowing it.'

I didn't have time to make sure he'd understood because some mad student was trying to interest me in his plan to shoot LSD over everyone through his acid gun. I advised him to consult Jay and looked round for the next question. Instead I had to go and dance for the cameras, while the DJ crooned immoral suggestions to me over the top of a randy Stones track. He sighed and breathed heavily for me all evening over his microphone and once or twice I thought of locating the DJ's box. But I was after something more symbolic and looked towards the stage where a young German underground group were tuning up.

Jay and I were seated at a table and given charts to fill in with our scores for the twenty competitors. The dance floor was cleared and the group started playing as the young would-be groupies streamed past us with numbers plastered to their bodies. I was no longer in the spotlight and my mind flashed on Reginald Chatterton at a beauty contest. They danced and swivelled in front of us and I eliminated the ones with fixed smiles on their faces. Most of them were terribly mis-cast, and we finally chose a pale skinny girl trying to look like Mick Jagger. The prize was a weekend in London with Jay and he started to get to work immediately. Now that the focus had been diffused I was at the mercy of any inquisitive person who chose to stop and question me. I went to the ladies room for some equality and signed a book for the old woman on duty. I stared at myself in the mirror and met four other pairs of female eyes. I went back to the reserved area to find the publishing crowd making beery jokes. I focused my eyes on the group and blinkered out anybody trying to catch my attention while I thought about the lead guitarist and wondered whether I should make the effort. There wasn't much else to do. When the group finished playing I beckoned Wolfgang to sit next to me.

'See that guy with the long dark hair?' I pointed. 'I'd like him for tonight.'

Wolfgang nodded. 'So?' he asked.

'I want you to get him for me. And I don't want any trouble at the hotel this time.'

'I can fix the hotel for you, I'm sure of that,' Wolfgang hesitated, 'but what do you want me to say to him?'

'Ask him if he'd like to meet me, ask him to have a drink with me, something like that,' I suggested.

'Why don't you do it? You have the experience, no?' He laughed.

'I'm shy,' I said, 'tonight.'

'So,' he said, 'I'll ask him if he's free for you.'

'Try to be subtle,' I said anxiously.

'No time for that,' he said, and strode towards the stage.

I watched him confer with the guitarist, who threw a startled look in my direction. I should have given a wink and wave, but pretended not to notice. Wolfgang reported back that he would be joining me in a few minutes. I basked in the reflection of this reversal of roles and waited for my tender victim. Axel was very friendly but could hardly speak English. There was no point in talking so I made him understand we were leaving and instructed Wolfgang to fix it. A car drove us to the hotel where we went through the farcical formality of registering Axel as my husband. The penguins on duty questioned Axel in poker-faced English. It was such a trite conspiracy that I giggled helplessly as I told them he spoke German.

'Ah, so!' they said, and all was settled with a lot of knowing nods and glances.

Face to face with him I didn't know where to begin.

'Why did you come with me?' I asked.

'To see what the girl under all the shit publicity is really like,' he said, and his English seemed to have improved. 'I couldn't speak before,' he explained, 'it was all too strange.'

'It was strange for me too,' I said, 'to do something like that.'

'I'm glad you did,' he said, 'I'm sure you're not really like that. I'm sure you're really very nice.'

When he had reassured me enough and the roles gradually re-reversed we tuned into some German jigs on the radio and switched on the vibrating bed. I had hoped for the moving train effect, but it just made us wobble like jellies. I was impressed by Axel's agility as he leap from position to position like a chunky gazelle, his long hair flying up and down.

'You *are* nice,' he kept saying, 'underneath it all,' and I responded to his vigour. At six in the morning he wanted to take me walking in the English Gardens to see the frosty daybreak. It was cold and I was tired and I had to make an attempt at being bright by noon to do some television. He accused me of playing the star and I felt ashamed and let the whole thing take a romantic turn. He insisted on taking me to the rehearsal cellar so he could play his guitar to me and romance was more an epilogue as I sat on the inevitable drum kit and listened to the same old riff. When we came to leave, Axel found he had locked us in and it would have made an appropriate coffin for me. We shouted but no one came, then Axel picked the lock.

'I used to be a burglar,' he told me.

Back in the daytime our roles were reversed again and he followed me through the interviews like the best of groupies. He would sit in a corner quietly until it was time to come and hold my hand and I would kiss him when I got bored with answering questions.

Jay was pursuing Wolfgang's secretary, having put Miss Super-Groupie into storage in deference to the older women he was doing so well with in Germany.

'I've never fancied older women before,' he confessed, 'because I didn't realise they'd have to be fantastic in bed. And far less complicated, you know.'

I thought of all the hysterical teenagers he was always complicating his life with and agreed with him. A German film star gave me a tapestry handbag and I gave Axel my Oliver Twist velvet cap before we said goodbye. He put it on proudly and set off to let his manager know he was still alive. Jay and I flew back to our own kind of reality.

11

I spent several days in bed with my sleeping rag and *The Electric Kool-Aid Acid Test* to blot Germany out of my mind. Jay and I found we were almost broke, and the film deal still hadn't happened.

While Jay and I were preparing for America, Atmos and Alice had decided to spend the summer in Ibiza, holiday-camp for full-on hippies. It was all free love and clap, well water and candles, shitting in the ground and tripping on the beach. Most freaks pass through Ibiza in one or several of their lives, though Ibiza now struck me the same as Zen did in '67: a bandwagon to be avoided. I imagined it full of Americans who had fallen off the Californian coastline bubbling freak argot and doing nothing about anything.

On the last night we were to have a farewell dinner together. Jay had pushed Mason to the back of his mind in the excitement of buying up Mr Freedom and a Gucci bag to put it all into. I had lots of flimsy tat and velvet to shimmer around in and felt an old leather suitcase was more my basket. I was into my packing when the evening rush hit me. Alice came into my room to try on some new clothes and found me collapsed beside my suitcase. I explained my position and she decided to join me. Soon we were giggling and dressing each other for dinner and already getting sentimental about our separation.

We went into the front room and did a fashion parade for Atmos. Alice told him she'd dropped some acid, and he said what a good idea. I'd never seen Atmos trip before and kept a corner of my eye on him. As he went up he also seemed to deflate slightly into the cushions and temporarily lost control of his magic vibe. The sight of Atmos so helpless turned Alice and me, already riding our high, into a couple of teasing shrews. However, when the phone rang and it was Jay wanting to know where and when we were meeting him, and could I pick up a pair of tapestry trousers he was having tapered, I was the mindless one. My appetite was of no importance, but the ritual of eating out with Alice and Atmos so high persuaded me to attempt some kind of organisation.

Two hours and eight people later, we managed to find a basement bistro where we could pretend to be inconspicuous. After the meal we careered round London in somebody's van saying goodbye to everyone we could think of. It was four in the morning before we were back where we started, Atmos, Alice and I.

'It's already tomorrow,' I said.

'Oh, we'll miss you,' wailed Alice, 'and when you get back we'll be gone too.'

'I don't know when I'll be back,' I said, 'I'm going to find Larry, you know.'

'Bring him back with you,' Alice said. 'I'll like him if he's an Aquarius.'

'Don't get lost finding him,' said Atmos, 'we've grown used to you around.'

'There are lots of others,' I said.

'It's not the same,' said Alice, 'I know where I am with you.'

Atmos pulled her across his knee and smacked her helpless bottom. She squealed in delight.

'What have I done?' she cried, 'have I said something naughty?'

'Greedy and conservative,' Atmos told her, 'nothing's ever the same.'

'I suppose not,' she sighed wistfully, 'but Tiptree is a special friend.'

'I know,' Atmos ruffled my hair, 'underneath the icy barriers.'

'What icy barriers?' I asked intrigued.

'Oh, the dispassionate person you pretend to be. The way you look without seeing and listen without hearing when you first meet somebody. It's a cold impression you give off at the beginning, though I know better now.'

'Not as well as you'd like to, I'm afraid,' I said, for I was sorry I had been unable to sleep with them.

'That doesn't matter now,' said Atmos, 'I was probably out of time. It seems to work fine as it is.'

'Keep thinking like that and I'll soon want to change your mind,' I told him. 'You know how it goes.'

'I'm beginning to get the rules,' he said, and went and put on the Triad song of three lovers into one won't go but why not? We all sat thinking about it and wondering if we'd missed the opportunity.

'She has two fellows,' said Alice about the song. 'Why can't I have two lovers to indulge my fancy instead of having to share you?'

'Because life isn't fair,' Atmos told her.

'I've never fucked my father,' I told them, 'I mean, most chicks can blame their hang-ups on being fucked by their fathers. Why haven't I been fucked by my father?'

'Because that's your hang-up,' said Atmos. 'You're looking for the father you've never fucked. Alice has found hers.' He tweaked her tits. 'Silly little things,' he told her.

'But I'm looking for my brother lover too,' I said.

'Maybe that's Jay.' suggested Alice.

'And Mason's my father and I don't sleep with either of them. I want a package-deal lover,' I said. 'Larry's got to be all-in-one.'

'See you in Ibiza,' joked Atmos.

'I'm serious,' I told him, 'is that so funny? And I'm going to let you into another secret; the man I give up my rag for is the *one*.'

'Is that the rag you're always looking for?' asked Alice. 'What is it?'

'I've had it since the beginning. My mother gave it to me because she didn't want me to suck my thumb. I've tried to give it up but I can't.'

'Has it been the same one all the time?' she asked.

'Oh no, I've lost them and thrown them away, and sometimes wash them, though they get this special smell that makes me high. And they have to be in the same material. My mother cuts them from my father's old pyjamas.'

'*Your father's old pyjamas* …?' Atmos asked slowly.

'Yes, they're flannel.'

'I know, but… *your father's pyjamas*!' Atmos emphasised.

'My father's pyjamas,' I repeated. 'Do I realise what I've just said? That rag is the answer to all my sublimation. Larry will release me.'

'But if he loves you he won't ask you to give it up,' said Alice.

'That's right,' I said, 'I can use my rag as a love-meter. If I love him enough I'll make myself give it up.'

'What do you do with it?' she asked.

'I hold it to my face and I breathe in …' I put my hands up and inhaled deeply. 'A couple of those and I'm half-way removed. Then I rub it round my mouth and between my fingers at the same time …' I rubbed my thumb across my lips and closed my eyes to imagine the effect. 'That removes me totally and I'm somewhere like in meditation. I loose contact with my body and sometimes rub my lips raw. And look at my finger.' I showed them a callous on my forefinger. 'I stick this in my mouth while all the rest is going on. I used the rag to hide it from my mother, but she didn't really mind as long as it wasn't my thumb.'

Atmos and Alice stared at me.

'That's incredible,' said Atmos.

'I want to see it,' said Alice.

I hesitated, for I had never shown it willingly to anybody. But they were special friends and it was our last night, and this would be my memento to them. I fetched the centre of attraction from the top of my suitcase and held it up, pathetic and crumpled in the candlelight.

'Does it have a name?' asked Atmos.

'Just sleeping rag. I used to cal it guy-guy.'

'Let me hold it.' Alice reached out her hand.

I handed it to her gingerly. She held it in cupped hands and looked at it seriously. Then she pressed it to her face and sniffed, delicately at first and then more deeply. She opened her eyes into mine.

'It smells of you,' she said, and handed it to Atmos. I watched him do the same and I thought how much closer we'd got than by fucking. He handed the rag back to me with reverence and I respected the intimacy I'd granted them. There wasn't time to go any further because the dawn was coming and I wasn't going to miss this plane. Only time – at last – to ask Atmos what the 'P' stood for.

'Phere,' he said, 'as in Atmosphere.'

12

A Bodhisattva from the 8th century stood stoned on an open lotus draped in flowing Grecian robes. The Blue Fudo glared from a cloud of fire over his kingdom of mythical creatures thrashing in the sky. A seventh Buddha of the Past dressed in a large halo with pearl-studded streamers was on his way to Valhalla. The Goddess of Compassion and Mercy, looking like a voluptuous hippy, was being attended by minor divinities and emblems, and Queen Candraprabha had come to visit. A four-armed three-headed deity sat cross-legged for ever, while the dragons chased their tails and the Divine Archer shot endlessly at the symbolical apple. There was a lot happening in the Duke's daughter's temple, and the incense smoked and the bongoes thudded, high over the warehouses down in the Bowery.

I had been in New York for two weeks and my cosmic plan was well under way. The astronauts were lost in space and Mr Nixon had found Cambodia so the American media had little time for groupies. It wasn't the kind of thing the silent majority wanted to know about; quiz games and soap operas kept them happy. The talk shows were terrified of losing their ratings and that was a pretty rigid kind of censorship to try and break through. The whole thing was a glorious misunderstanding and our American publishers wanted to forget about us as soon as possible. Jay was furious at the mis-handling of our non-event, and when we were asked to leave the grand hotel and fend for ourselves, we combined vocal chords to demand financial assistance. Our insistent bleating paid off, and Jay left for Los Angeles to chase the mythical film deal. He had assumed that I would want to go with him, but I couldn't. I had yet to locate Larry, and now had the time to start. With one phone number I traced my way through agents, managers and friends, all telling me different stories. I spent hours trying to locate him in the Bellevue hospital files. Finally I managed to find his closest friend, Lee, who seemed to know me well. He had a high-class address for Larry in LA with a wheedle-proof phone number and I wondered if he'd scored himself a rich lady, or even if he remembered me. It was nearly a year ago since I'd received a mad letter with no address except a drawing of a square house surrounded by railings. I expressed a brief note to him and tried to forget while I waited.

I had Tommy to love me and his quaint apartment in the Village to stay in. Tommy was a romantic and we got on fine, talking chick-shit like the best of ladies. We both seemed to live in the perpetual cliché, and of course he loved me because I loved another. I tried to love him in that other way, broadly speaking, but my mind wasn't on it and my body turned away. He took me round the social sights and kept me well out of my mind, and it was through the clearness of cocaine I stared at the temple walls. With a mind sledgehammered by psychedelics, I had found the subtlety of cocaine slow to realise. I felt it was another drug for another time that I hadn't reached yet or wasn't ready for. I didn't want my destiny diverted by tangents. My fantasy of Larry sustained itself on a diet of psilocybin until the Great Bell Telephone in the sky turned him into a voice that I wouldn't have recognised if I'd heard it in my sleep.

I'd just got high for an evening at Nobodys when the phone rang. No surprise, probably for Tommy.

'It's for you,' he said.

'Hello, it's Larry …' and of course that blew a few fuses.

'It's Larry …' he's real, I've found him, what am I going to say, this is what I've been waiting for…

'Wow, hello,' I said. My nervous system was shaking so I sat down and I could feel Tommy watching me so I was playing for two audiences and there was myself as well. I couldn't remember a word I said, and rushed to the bedroom and fell on the bed wailing in delight when it was all over. Tommy stood in the doorway waiting.

'He's got a bad cold,' I giggled hysterically. 'But he wants to see me. Immediately. It's happening. I knew it was going to. I'm so happy.' Tommy looked wistful. 'And I'm so frightened,' I said.

Tommy understood, and let me talk about Larry all night. I never even kissed him goodbye the morning I found myself crying in the pouring rain on Sheridan Square with not a yellow cab to be had and a plane to be missed. The panic was real but unnecessary, for the plane had engine trouble and we had four hours of free drinks to wait through. I sent a corny postcard to Atmos and Alice saying I'm leaving on a jet plane, don't know when I'll be back again, and brooded over a vodka about the interim phone calls Larry and I had tortured ourselves with in a vain attempt to explain everything. There were moments when it seemed all too much for him, and the commitment he was attempting over the wires would weigh him down into a depression. I had been warned about his withdrawals by Lee, who had insisted on seeing me before I saw Larry, to explain things I should know about him before I declared myself. Lee knew how Larry had felt about me, and wanted to know how I felt about Larry. The description of his madness frightened me and made me feel inadequate to cope; I was the one who needed saving. We would save each other, I vowed, and what could be more worthwhile? Lee seemed satisfied with that.

To learn I was a groupie who had written about it, and more than that, sacrificed and even distorted our personal secret, caused Larry grave concern. He had rushed out to buy a copy of the book immediately to read about himself and hadn't liked it.

'Not even the elastic band?' I teased hopefully.

'I don't remember that bit,' he said. 'Those letters you had me write, are those the sort of things you imagined of me?'

'There was this other American musician whom I juxtaposed with you,' I explained. 'To kind of disguise you.'

'I hardly recognise myself,' he complained. 'I suppose that explains it. Why didn't you leave it as it was?'

I thought I had. 'You went barmy, didn't you?' I joked. 'I didn't know that when I wrote it.

'Don't say things like that,' he said, 'unless you're being funny.'

'I was,' I said.

When I thought how guardedly I had told his story in comparison to the outright cruelty bestowed on some other characters I racked my principles in despair. Madness had been an obvious conclusion to a thwarted romance and it must have been in the air for me to think of it. It was too heavy for him that I had anticipated his condition, however inaccurately I had portrayed it.

'It was Paul McCartney I turned into, not Dylan,' he explained.

'But Dylan was this other guy's thing, that's the only reason.'

I didn't approve of his choice of re-identity. Dylan seemed more worthwhile than Paul McCartney. I told myself not to be snobbish and ordered another vodka. Paul McCartney probably had some hidden secret only Larry knew about. I was confident I would understand it too.

'I've been through some changes since I last saw you,' he had kept telling me. 'I may not be what you expect.'

'Have you thought that I might not be what you expect either? I've changed too,' I told him.

'I think I know what to expect,' he said, 'that's why I'm worried about myself.'

His troubled spirit disturbed me, for I couldn't reassure him, and he would start cursing the distance between us that inhibited communication.

'It'll be different when we can see each other,' I said.

'My hair isn't long any more,' he told me.

'What a pity,' I said, 'how about your moustache?'

'Oh, that's still here. I just hope my hair isn't too short. It's over my collar, though,' he added.

'Mine's red now, and I'll be wearing purple boots with silver stars,' I said, 'in case you don't recognise me.'

When the plane was in the air and there was no turning back I wondered whether fantasies could only be perfect in the mind. Lee had told me how much there was in Larry to love and how hard Larry might make it for me. I allowed myself to be so brought down that I took to my sleeping rag and just stared blankly at the enormous land beneath that looked like a geography lesson.

Over the Rockies I left the pressurised cabin and was down there in the 1850s, riding groupie to the bandits. It was a long trance, until suddenly I realised that Los Angeles was next and I dashed to the toilet so I could be back in my seat for the entrance over the end of the world. But synchronisity misplaced me, for when I returned I found the barren sea of mountains had become an everlasting game of Monopoly that shone and glittered in all directions, as though nothing else had ever existed. Microdots moved on the roads in precise formation and the whole complex looked like a transistorised memory circuit. I couldn't believe there were humans down there until the looking-glass effect slowly reversed and shapes took their programmed identities and I looked down at my feet to see if my boots were still purple and had silver stars.

13

'I'm sorry I'm late,' I announced, stopping in front of the young man in blue denim reading *Newsweek*. I wasn't quite sure, but when he looked up I knew the eyes. He smiled at me slowly and stood up.

'That's all right,' he said, 'I got drunk.'

Then we kissed and hugged and set off with our arms around each other like I've seen other lovers do when they meet at airports. He drove a white automatic sports car, and I took my boots off and crossed my legs for my first ride into Los Angeles. Larry turned on the FM radio so we didn't have to say too much and I glanced at him sideways to check his features. I hadn't ever thought of him visually during our separation and had no idea whether I found him physically attractive. I must have then, so I still do, I told myself, and turned my attention to the Hollywood mansions behind their trees and railings. On Sunset Strip the billboards dominated my vision, and Larry told me it took about a week to get over their impact. Liberace, ten times larger than life in a gold sequined suit glittered down at us with an oily smirk, advertising his appearance in Las Vegas. Pop groups were on prominent display with their latest releases, and movies made and movies coming that I'd never heard of reminded me that I was in the city of the stars, past, present and future imperfect. Under the cardboard monsters I spotted bare-footed freaks and psychedelic shop-fronts beginning to blend uneasily under the baleful eye of the over-sized cops. Then we wound our way up Laurel Canyon, passing charming little wooden houses nestling in the rocks until we came to our own hacienda high on the hill, roses and all.

'This can be your home if you like,' Larry told me. 'So just arrange yourself how you want.'

There was a sturdy simplicity in the beams and wooden floors, and the furniture was comfortable. We moved the mattress from the bedroom in front of the open fire between the speakers and the television, for that would be the centre of our universe. Larry sat on the sofa rolling while I scattered my belongings and draped the shawls I had brought to cope with hotel environment.

So the scene was set and the smoke was lit.

'We've got to be up front with each other,' he told me. 'I couldn't bear to think you were playing a game.'

'We've had this discussion before,' I said. 'When I say games I mean everything is a game, the only choice is how to play it.'

'All right, then I'm asking you to play this game fairly, if you must call it a game. I call games mind-fucking.'

'So do I,' I said, 'it can't be helped.'

'I can't afford to lose my mind again. I'm just asking you to understand that.'

'I don't want you to lose your mind,' I said.

'Then be up front with me and tell me what you want.'

I took a deep breath. 'I wanted to see you again to see if I wanted to see you for ever, I suppose.'

'You couldn't forget me.'

'No.'

'I felt the same about you.' He turned and held my hand. 'I've wanted to see you all this time, but like I tried to explain in my letters, all these things kept happening to me.'

He told me how he'd left the group to concentrate on recording and engineering techniques, which had always fascinated him.

'It's far more interesting to manipulate that kind of

machinery than it is to play the same tunes over and over again to people who don't listen anyway. And it requires more skill.'

'What about your music?' I asked, trying not to let his image wilt.

'I've still got that,' he said, 'though I can't quite write the kind of tunes I'd like to yet. My ambition is to do what Paul did, make a totally solo album.'

Then he played me Paul McCartney playing himself on everything, and it just didn't turn me on.

'He's not a drummer,' I had to observe.

'Perhaps not, but don't you appreciate the overall achievement? That's all him, the heart and soul of the man. I know what he's been through.'

He was quite worked up, and it distressed me not to be able to share his enthusiasm. What did I care about Paul McCartney? It seemed I would have to try.

'What's he been through?' I asked.

'Listen to those words. I had a tape of all his songs that I played again and again until I understood.'

'Understood what?'

'That he was trying to get in touch with me. That's when I started going strange and became possessed by him. I can't imagine how it happened, but there must have been a reason. Although I'm myself again now I enjoy his music so much because I've been him and understood his soul.'

There seemed a kind of logic in that, except that in my book it would have been mystical romance with George Harrison instead of Shetland pullovers with Linda and Paul. So I understood but couldn't agree, and felt confused at having to pretend when I was supposed to be Up Front. It shouldn't have upset Larry that I wasn't crazy about Paul McCartney but I knew it would, so I deceived him, by his analysis.

He sketched in the details of what he could remember, for

the drugs given to suppress his schizophrenia had caused some amnesia and vegetablisation of the brain.

'I can still feel what they did to me. My mental reflexes aren't as fast as they should be, though I'm improving,' he said encouragingly. 'But I can get bogged down, and that's terribly frustrating.'

'What does it feel like?' I asked.

'There's a link missing,' he explained, 'knowing something without being able to explain it.'

'That sounds familiar.'

'It's more than that,' he said, 'I'm having to work out things I know already.'

'I'm doing that all the time.'

'I know what you mean, but the difference is that when you've worked it out then you find you know it. These are issues I had sorted out before, I've already got the answer but can't remember how. My though processes have been confused.'

'Sounds like an overdose,' I said.

'Something like that.'

Only he hadn't been taking any acid when he flipped and hadn't dared to since. I told him how I'd been taking a lot of acid to dissociate myself from my identity, for whatever it was, I found it easier to have none. He was inquisitive about the way I functioned under a continual intake of low dosage, and wondered whether it would help him to try. It was difficult to know, and somehow I couldn't be too enthusiastic.

'Most people I know who take a lot of acid have had their brains turned to cheese,' Larry said.

'I sometimes wonder whether I'm real without acid,' I said. 'So I have to stop from time to time to get some identity back to play with.'

He wanted to see me on acid, and I promised I'd be taking some tomorrow. I was too spaced out on jet lag and everything else to need anything more than a downer, and I turned

Larry on with my psychic favourite that makes everything rosy. Our future soon looked warm and secure, and so did the bed.

Whatever memory I'd had of his loving, he far exceeded it. His body was pale and slight, but certainly not frail. He vigorously devoted his attention to my pleasure, and all I had to do was lie there and enjoy it. Whatever I did to him, he seemed more interested in doing it to me, so I let him. It made some kind of change that kept making my mind wander, and that didn't seem to matter either. I could still enjoy my body and slip into an all-too-easy orgasm whenever I felt like it, which I actually had to control if I was to sustain him. He seemed to know all my favourite secrets and I hoped the communication between our bodies would help break the shadowy misunderstandings of our minds.

This was the thought I clung to when the fear started to get hold of me the following evening. I had dropped a controllable amount of acid because I had a premonition of confusion. But though I felt the drug physically, my mind failed to receive the usual sparkle. Instead, Larry seemed to be intercepting the energy and directing me somewhere I didn't want to go. We were talking about ourselves again, and I could hear myself answering him like an interview, knowing that everything I said sounded different to him than it did to me, for he had been programmed by his cosmic pattern to interpret everything the way he wanted.

'There's something more than us... don't you feel it, something that makes us do the things we do, like you finding me, like us meeting in the first place... something more than us... you do feel it, don't you...?' and he was raising his voice and clutching my arm, his eyes shining into mine with the hint of madness that Lee had described.

'Sometimes I feel it, sometimes I don't,' I sounded non-committal and tried to explain. 'I want to believe, that's what I've come for, but there's always been something holding me back. It's more than rationalisation, I'm useless at logic, it's something I can't identify and don't like.'

'It's fear,' he said, 'I never want you to be frightened of me.'

That made it worse. I felt the acid in me and the madness in him produced a negative reaction that held its own peculiar horror. I felt Larry was demanding total vision of my mind and my soul. He couldn't allow that I was the only one allowed to judge myself, and instinct defended my rights accordingly. So he found me evasive and inconsistent, and I remembered how open and revealing I enjoyed being, all that Larry wanted, but I had told Tommy more truths in New York than I felt I'd ever be able to tell this fantasy soul-mate. Tommy had said he thought we all knew too much about each other and being Up Front was just another mind-fuck.

Larry didn't disguise his dislike of my behaviour with guys since he'd last seen me. He found something distasteful in the way I had written blatantly about my experiences, and managed to make me feel guilty.

'You won't go on like that when you're with me, will you?' he asked.

'I can promise,' I said, 'but I can't promise to keep my promise.'

He looked distressed and I felt resentful.

'I shouldn't have to promise,' I said. 'I mean, you shouldn't have to ask me.'

'I know, I know,' he said, shaking his head. 'But it would really upset me. I suppose I wouldn't mind occasionally. But not all the time, I just couldn't stand it.'

'It's my job,' I teased him. 'I'll have nothing to write about.'

'Why can't you write about other things? Why can't you make stories up like other writers?'

'I don't know,' I said, 'I'm not really a writer.'

'It would be more creative,' he encouraged, 'and I'll be

earning enough to look after you. I don't want you to write about things like that.'

'I'll write about you and me living together and what it's like.'

'Do you have to?' he asked dubiously. 'I'd find it very disturbing. Even though you've explained the other things you wrote, it still makes me feel strange to know that some of me is in print.'

'I'm joking,' I said, 'I may never write another book.'

'Oh, you must,' he said, 'and it's wrong of me to tell you what not to do; I suppose I'm being selfish.'

He smiled at me.

'But I feel selfish about you,' he started kissing me. 'I want you all for myself, isn't that how it's meant to be?'

'Yes,' I said.

He started on about destiny and all the complications we had to overcome, but we'd be strong enough, and how I'd come and live with him in LA because he would be working here for a while, then we'd move somewhere else, I'd like Boston, he said, and it would be nice to go back to London sometime because he'd really liked it there, and I'd probably miss my friends. I missed them already, and felt trapped. But I managed to suppress my negative feelings because they were annoying me, and I made myself believe in him. It worked for three days and then I got in touch with Jay.

14

'How are you enjoying LA?' Jay quizzed me from behind his outsize health drink.

'I haven't been around much yet,' I said. 'I only arrived four days ago.'

'Where have you been?'

'Up in the hills,' I said. 'With Larry.'

Jay looked at me intently.

'Yes… how is Larry?'

'We're in love,' I said defiantly.

'Well, it's lasted three days longer than I predicted,' he said.

'Why do you always say things like that?' I demanded. 'This is very serious.'

Jay's expression became sincere.

'I know exactly how serious it is – both of you building your hopes up like this – I just hope you're not going to be unkind to him. Let him down gently.'

'But I'm supposed to be staying with him… for ever …' I protested feebly.

'Come on now,' he chided, 'we all know about your little games.'

I glared at him, and felt discouraged.

'Anyway,' he looked at me sternly, 'while you've been romancing in the hills I've been checking out the film deal.'

'How is it?'

'You may well ask. The script is half-way done and reads like a conducted tour round Trendsville. Apparently you talked to the guy when we was in London and he couldn't understand a word you said.'

'I'm too far out.'

'You're too stoned.' Jay sounded reproving.

'He's too straight.'

'Whatever, you're not going to like yourself in it.'

'Am I plastic?'

'Afraid so.'

'What about the deal?'

'It's all over the place. I phoned Mason and find he's on holiday. He's got no business taking holidays when he should be here getting our deal together. And I told him so when I got through to him in the Bahamas.'

'What did he say?'

'He hung up on me.'

'What are you going to do, then?'

'Well, I'm going to find myself a red-hot lawyer and let him sort Mason out. He's broken his contract and I want the property back.'

'What will you do with it?'

'I'll sell it myself. And I'd advise you to do the same.'

All that money at stake and I had to make a decision. If I acted with Jay the inevitable litigation would delay any deal forever. If I stuck with Mason I rendered Jay's decision pretty futile. I decided to do both.

Larry came by to pick me up and to meet Jay for the first time. They were extremely polite to each other and I could see that Larry was impressed by Jay's charm. We arranged to meet Jay later at the Whiskey with some people he'd picked up since he'd been in LA.

'Jay's very nice,' Larry told me.

'You wouldn't think he was a ponce, would you?' I asked, wanting to shock.

'He seems very honest to me,' Larry said.

'He does, doesn't he? Only some people don't see it, and

think he's a ponce.'

'Well, you should know. What do you think?' asked Larry.

'If he's a ponce, then I'm a tart,' I told him, 'people like to think the worst.'

'I don't understand what you mean,' Larry was troubled. 'I don't know what you want me to think.'

'I want you to think it's a joke,' I said, 'I want you to laugh at it all. America takes itself too seriously.'

'I laugh at myself,' he insisted, 'but it's a kind of down humour that never reaches my face. I know I look serious, yes, I am serious, but I'm laughing as well.'

He looked at me hopefully.

'Well, that's all right then,' I said, 'but when I make jokes you seem to get confused and sad.'

'That's difficult to explain,' he said, 'I suppose it's because the things I find funny about you are the things that I fear will separate us.'

I knew what he meant and got brought down with him. I spent the rest of the afternoon amusing myself with a letter to Cy Henry, and wishing Larry wouldn't stare at me, for it inhibited my emotional discharge. I knew he wanted to read it, but I was supposed to show it to him, for he couldn't ask.

There was more high drama when a chick who had been loving him for a year had to be told.

'She thinks I'm going to live with her, and I suppose I would have, if you hadn't turned up.'

'Does she have to know immediately?' I asked.

'The sooner she knows, the sooner she can get over it,' he said practically.

'If I was her I wouldn't want to know,' I said.

'She's got her suspicions,' he said, 'I've spoken about you.'

'Then you don't have to tell her.'

'I've got to be fair to her. And I'd like you to be with me

when I phone her. You'd actually like each other,' he added foolishly.

'Send her my love,' I said.

Larry gave me a wan smile. 'I'm sorry,' he said, 'you don't have to listen.'

But I wanted to punish myself for this whole state of affairs, and sat calmly through the two-way death sentence. When it occurred to me what was really happening I wanted to giggle. I moved closer to him and took his hand. I smiled up at him, and told him silently he was a fool. I felt a dreadful rush of power and lay back listening to the gruesome charade which couldn't be anything to do with me, for I was nothing more than a pawn in a rather bad joke. I might as well just play the part until it was time to move on.

A blast from the past confronted us in the Whiskey in the unmistakable form of Reginald Chatterton. He'd been in town some weeks in pursuit of hot glossy news and had met up with Jay on the Hollywood grapevine. He was pretty spaced out on something, he told me proudly he was taking all kinds of dope now, had caught the clap twice since he'd been here, and tried to persuade Jay to come to a wife-swapping party. He roared with laughter a lot, and fidgeted nervously on his chair. He tried to engage me in a dirty joke repartee, but I could feel Larry stiff beside me, and concentrated most of my attention on the group of stage.

'I like watching musicians,' I said afterwards.

'I could always join a band again,' Larry said. 'I've had plenty of good offers. It's just that I feel past stage-performing.'

'Don't worry about it,' I told him. 'You should do what you want.'

'I'd like to please you as well whenever possible,' he said.

He continued to please me in bed more than I could believe and the ambiguous way in which I loved him puzzled me. We had our best fucks when we'd reached the limit of our misunderstanding, when there was nothing left to do but to end it all or fuck. Neither of us had the courage to end it, and our love-making was the only thing we had left of our convictions. It was a relief to decide that Jay and I should return to London and get our papers sorted out by a lawyer to confront Mason on his return. My convictions returned enough to be able to promise Larry I would come back when everything was sorted out and I had enough money not to think for a while. He wanted to believe me, and said he'd work and wait, and if I made him wait too long he might just come over and fetch me.

'I'd love an excuse to come to London again,' he said.

'We'll work out what's best in our letters,' I said.

He looked serious. 'You must understand something,' he said, 'I find it very hard to write letters. That's why my communications have been so erratic in the past. But I promise I'll try and think of something to say, even if I don't understand it myself.'

'Well, I'll enjoy writing to you,' I said. 'All I need to know is where you are.'

We went through the formality of writing each other's addresses into our little black books and amongst my psychedelic souvenirs of California I managed to smuggle out some grape-flavoured Joy-Jel for future pleasures unknown. I also had time to fix myself up with a couple of Big Studio luncheons with movie guys I'd met with Mason, for I had to have done something glamorous in such a city. But stars look anonymous these days and films are shot mostly on location, and I felt like I was eating in a rather deserted factory canteen.

Most of my memories were left in the double bed in front of the fire, where I learnt about America from the twenty-four-hour tube and listened to stereo late at night. I saw David Frost sell his soul for a suit and I learnt Ralph Williams second-hand car slogans off by heart. There was no escape from advertisements, and the damage they did to the concentration gradually impaired the health of the brain until it couldn't tell the difference. I had little contact with the Californian consciousness cult except to exchange stars (and cults) with various freak neighbours. On the day before I was due to leave they came to tell me I had passed the Unconscious Community Vibe Test, and the local Astral Agent presented me with a free horoscope in coloured crayons. They were sorry I was leaving so soon after being voted into their community, and hoped I would return.

'I just hope it won't be another two years in the pattern before I see you again,' Larry said ruefully, as we settled in for the last night.

'Let me sleep tonight,' I said, 'we can outwit last night dramas by never having one.'

Larry looked very hurt.

'I want every memory I can get,' he said, so I let him have just one more little one. He looked at me sadly for a long time afterwards.

'I just have to accept that certain things I want from you will have to remain unexpressed in my own head,' he said, and kissed me softly on the forehead. Then he sat by the fire and hummed to his guitar while he watched me sleep. When I stirred in my dreams he placed the stray sleeping rag in my hands in devotional duty. He stayed with me right up to the Departure Lounge, though I was long gone before.

15

After we'd told our tale and shown the evidence to the lawyer we were told to keep out of Mason's way and let it run through legal channels. With that off my mind there was nothing I wanted to do except brood out a new kind of logic for myself. So I retreated as far as I could into myself and spent a week with my parents in the country. Whatever they felt inwardly about the content of the book, they had forgiven me outwardly, and my mother came to fetch me. I'd had no sleep the night before, I'd been drawn into a wild fantasy of a new political party by a couple of young revolutionaries, and went without sleep in the hope of being convinced that someone could save the world. I wanted to talk to my mother to keep myself awake, but we were driving through her childhood country, which was now suburban and hard to imagine, so I filtered everything off by falling into a disguised drowse. They had a new house that I hadn't been to before, though it wasn't quite as isolated as I'd hoped. But there were woods I could hide in and the sun was shining so it was all quite balmy.

At dinner my father asked me what wine I wanted to drink, Hock or Burgundy? My culture hadn't extended beyond knowing the difference between Black Pak and Nepalese, Turkish and Moroccan.

'Vote Conservative,' he urged me. 'Save the country from these wretched Socialists.'

'I can't,' I said, 'not with any conscience.'

'Do you think those Trade Unionists have an conscience?'

he asked. 'They just want to nationalise everything for themselves.'

'Works both ways,' I said.

'But that Mr Wilson looks so creepy,' my mother said.

'And Mr Heath is a man of principle,' I said.

'I'd like to see Home up there myself,' said my father.

'I always thought Anthony Eden looked such a nice man,' said my mother, 'but your father prefers Macmillan as a politician.'

'They're all the same,' I said, 'just choose the one whose tricks suit you best.'

My father looked at me sternly. 'No wonder Britain is going to the dogs,' he complained. 'Do all your friends think like that?'

'More so,' I said, 'I'm a very passive revolutionary.'

'What I want to know is,' demanded my mother, 'what all you so-called revolutionaries will do to make everything better when all you have to do is vote Conservative.'

'That only makes it better for the Capitalists.'

'Well, if that's what you call people who work for a living, why not?' demanded my father. 'Why should I support layabouts who are just too lazy to go out to work?'

'Quite agree,' I said, 'that's why I'm not going to pay income tax.'

That really shocked them. That was stealing from the country. It never paid to make an outrageous remark to them for I always ended up reassuring them I didn't mean it. My father wanted a complete breakdown of my financial position and thought I was very careless not to know how much I had earned down to the last penny. Their lives were so neat and orderly that my haphazard attitudes confused them. My dear mother, saving on housekeeping by shopping for reduced 'lines' in food, still wanted to make my bed and run my bath and do my washing, an expression of the love that stopped physically when at the age of eight she told me I was too old to kiss her.

I kept my mother company in the kitchen and she would gossip to me about the family and neighbours.

'One of Mr Linstrom's sons had a nervous breakdown,' she said, 'but some brave girl insisted on marrying him, even though it's bound to happen again.'

'I knew someone like that,' I said, 'but maybe she can help him.'

'I'm sure she will,' my mother agreed, 'she seemed a very nice girl. But what about her? He had to be taken away for quite a while, and I don't think it's a good idea to marry someone in a possible condition like that.'

I agreed with her that all abnormalities were hazardous and hoped she wouldn't notice my dilated pupils. My mother was worried that I had spoiled my chances of a decent marriage by writing such a book. I wondered if what I had been looking for in Larry was an updated version of my parents relationship – absolutely one for one, with my father strictly dominant and my mother accepting this as right and proper. It was a master/slave relationship of the most considerate kind, that basked in a strangely painless love. But Larry and I were both too crazy ever to be without the pain and the pain had been too much to bear, so I had to work out some kind of painless love. I hadn't been able to take acid since that night with Larry, but needed something now to fill the vacuum in my head, so I popped an MDA cap and scribbled all my problems in my notebooks. My parents thought my glassy vagueness was due to inspiration fighting its way out of my fingertips, and I liked the joke.

My mother was still knitting and reading historical romances while listening to *Your Hundred Best Tunes from the Past*. My father kept time to The March of Aida from behind *The Daily Telegraph* with a patriotic expression on his face. He asked me what newspaper I favoured and had never heard of *International Times* and thought *Rolling Stone* was a dirty rock group. He would read out any atrocity he could find to illustrate how misguided my political views were and I wished I had a more masculine kind of rhetoric to cope with his accusations. I read *Portnoy's Complaint* in bed and laughed about Mason being Jewish.

Although it was hard to feel anything about anybody, after a week I missed the action and had to return to my other orbit. My father drove me to the station and it was the only time we were alone. He tried for the last time to understand my ways by pressing me with questions on my future, and how I intended to plan for that old-age security that sensible people waste their lives providing for. I could give him nothing more than indefinite vagaries, and listened to his advice without accepting it. He knew the pattern from the wasted hours spent in his study trying to get at the truth of some petty misdemeanour. Then he had been able to stop my pocket money, now he could only sigh wearily.

'I don't know where we went wrong,' he said, and he'd never spoken like that before, 'I mean, your mother's a reasonable woman.'

'She's very good,' I said.

'The best,' he agreed, 'and I can't bear to see her worrying about you. I don't expect you to have any feelings for me, but I wish you'd think of your mother.'

'I think of both of you,' I said, 'but I still have to work everything out for myself.'

'But why, *why*?' he asked, 'when I was your age there was no more to it than to please my parents. I studied and worked to become something they could be proud of.'

'I don't live like this to spite you – I wouldn't *mind* you being proud of me, you know,' I said. 'But I'm just not good at the kind of things that make you proud, and I don't want to be ashamed about that.'

I couldn't get out of the cliché until I was safely alone in the train where nobody mattered except myself. More divided loyalties were waiting for me in London, and the final outrage between Jay and Mason. Jay had warned me that Mason would contact me to try and swing me back on to his side. Jay forbade me to allow this, and I tried to promise without commitment. I felt fatalistic about the whole situation, for somebody's trust would be betrayed. Mason had betrayed ours, and I was to betray Jay's. A dozen roses and a soft phone call was all the power Mason needed for me to see him secretly. Then I persuaded Jay to listen, just once more, for the last time.

'I'm here against my better judgment,' announced Jay. Mason was behind the oval desk all in black leather with his arms crossed. 'And against Tiptree's too, if she had a better judgment.' He looked at me scornfully.

'I'm responsible for that,' Mason was quick to defend me. 'I think you're behaving very foolishly and could spoil everything for yourselves with this petty disagreement.'

'It would certainly spoil everything for *you*,' said Jay. 'For you turned down a sum of money far from petty in the hope of getting another deal that was better for you and probably worse for us.'

Mason sighed a smile and leant forward.

'How many times do I have to explain?' he asked. 'I know it looks as though I'm wearing two hats over this deal, and perhaps I am, but believe me, however many hats I'm wearing, I'm wearing them in your *best interests*.'

'Save that one for Tiptree,' said Jay. 'You've lost your ring of confidence with me.'

Mason looked baffled and I could see Jay trembling with suppressed emotion. Then he cleared his throat.

'I can see only one solution,' Jay said, 'you can buy me out. Then you can screw it up as much as you want, because Tiptree won't notice if you keep her stoned enough. Will you?' he asked me lightly.

I was taken by surprise and could only roll my eyes.

'I'm sick of being treated like a money tree,' said Mason angrily. 'Buy you? I'd have to sell you to make any kind of profit. I've invested my own money in this deal to keep it going, you know.'

'That's your mistake,' said Jay, 'I'm not going to pay for that. So I'm going to fight you.'

He stood up to leave.

'You'll certainly pay if you do that,' said Mason, but Jay didn't answer and was gone.

'What about you?' Mason turned to me. I could feel tears pricking behind my eyes at all the bitterness.

'I think it's all revolting,' I said, 'and I'm extremely upset with both of you.'

'I'm sorry about that,' he said, 'but I have to know which way you want to go.'

'I want to go away,' I said, 'and never have to think about it again.'

'That's how it should be,' said Mason, 'so why don't you let me sort it all out? I can fix Jay if I know you'll behave.'

'You make it very difficult for me,' I said, 'because I'm half on his side too. So just get the deal and send us a cheque. If you don't then it's all over anyway.'

'Two weeks,' he said eagerly, 'I promise there'll be something in two weeks.'

'Another promise,' I said. 'Can you make me believe you?'

'What do you want me to say,' he asked me. 'I love you, you know.'

I bet he did, for getting his own way, but I kissed him goodbye pretending it was more than that, pretending it was a bond deeper than a piece of paper that held me to him.

16

It was midsummer in London and I found myself alone, body and soul. Jay had somehow disappeared, and a stoned letter for Ibiza made me miss my friends more than my lovers. I spent most of my time in my darkened room with my rag, just trying to think. But there was no one left to tell until Cy Henry rode back into town, with whom I'd struck up a non-fucking kind of friendship.

Cy had a lot of pads to bop around, but needed somewhere to dump his stuff and I told him he could use the box room for whatever he wanted while the others were away. He said my room was like a Buddhist whorehouse and my mind needed a dose of Wei Wu Wei.

'He's bound to be here somewhere,' I said, and indicated the inscrutable range of Eastern literature his lordship had left behind. I hadn't known where to start, but Cy recognised some old favourites and left me to adjust my libido. I realised yet again that my ego was the problem and here was a non-chemical solution. Old Chinese proverbs reduced everything to nonsense that made perfect sense like the best Owsley without the comedowns. Here was a format for thinking that could have made me the peaceful vegetable I thought I wanted to be if I'd known how to apply it. Cy answered my problems with ancient quotations to put me in perspective with infinity except he forgot to remind me I was a Westerner. He stayed in the box room more than I thought he would and explained it was like living in a womb and rather interesting. He dropped some acid one day and locked himself in. He burst into my room two hours later full of frustrated energy. I smiled at him over the top of my Li Po and quoted:

'I am a peach tree blossoming in a deep pit.
Who is there I may turn to and smile?
You are the moon up in the far sky;
Passing, you look down on me an hour; then
went on forever.'

'I'm not in the mood,' Cy told me sharply. 'I'm trying to have a bad trip.'

'What for?' I asked.

'Because I've never had one and I want to know what the horrors are like. I thought if I shut myself in a blank room with nothing to do I might get some grotesque hallucinations.'

'I can't think why,' I said.

'Because I'm bored,' he said, and turned on the television.

'Cocksucker!' he shouted at President Nixon's rubbery face making its excuses for South-Ease Asia, and turned the set off again.

'There's nothing I want to do,' he complained. 'Why can't I have a bad trip?'

'Maybe you are,' I said.

'Very funny,' he said scornfully, and disappeared back into his room. I dipped into my Krishnamurti reader and fell asleep. It was dark when I opened my eyes and Cy stood in front of me with a candle.

'I feel randy,' he announced.

'I'm asleep,' I said.

'Well, wake up,' he commanded.

'I don't feel like it.'

'You never do. What's the matter? Got the clap?'

'Just frightened of catching it,' I said.

'I'm not a pox star,' he said indignantly. Then he laughed at his joke and patted me paternally on the head.

'Doesn't matter,' he said, 'I can always find myself a bimbo. Two, if I feel like it.'

Slightly madder than Mason's white patent boot bimbos, but all after the same glitter, Cy's ladies would do anything out of the *Karma Sutra* just to keep jumping from Lear jet to private yacht with the right fashionable freaks. Some of them turned into real freaks along the way and took up crochet, and Alice was some kind of bimbo until she met Atmos. Cy had known her as a Bluebell dancer in New York before she'd turned on.

Cy disappeared for a week of social orgies and I waited for Mason's promise, but the phone hardly rang these days. Another raving letter from the good doctor and a crazy post-script from Alice convinced me to join them. I planned to lie on the roof of their country abode and saturate in the sun armed only with *A Geometric Concept of Love and Sex* to keep my love-beam impersonal.

'So it's come to that,' Cy remarked, when he returned to the box room for some privacy. He was already flexing his cards into fancy shuffles to show me a new trick.

'I'm only going for the sun,' I said.

'The great Ibizan drop out,' he said. 'Pick a card.' I drew the Queen of Hearts and giggled.

'So what?' I said, 'it's an experience.'

'Pick another card,' he said, 'I'm sure you'll have lots of experiences. You might never come back. Pick one more card and lay them face down in the order you selected them from left to right.'

'I don't think I could stand all that natural living for more than a couple of weeks,' I said, laying out the cards. 'But that'll be long enough to get a tan.'

Cy was staring intently at the back of the cards.

'Pick them up and replace them in the pack anywhere you want,' he instructed. 'If you want a tan, you should get your-self a ride on Ambrose Deacon's yacht. And you wouldn't have to worry about natural living either.'

When I'd finished he picked up the pack and flipped through it casually.

'I've never had to shit on the ground before,' I said. 'I'd like to give it a try.'

'Queen of Hearts, Knave of Diamonds, Two of Clubs,' he announced triumphantly, 'in that order.'

'You're right,' I said.

'There's another part, but I haven't worked it out yet.' He started arranging the cards in front of him.

'You're really very sheltered, aren't you?' he asked. 'You've never done the great Eastern trek.'

'I suppose I ought to,' I said. 'Just to see.'

'And to get bombed out,' he said. 'That's the best part. But it's better to fly there than walk, unless you're an American hippy, I suppose.'

'Well, I can only get as far as Ibiza this time,' I said, 'I've done as many countries as I can take this year.'

Cy was practising dealing from the bottom.

'Not bad going for starters,' he said. 'You'll be able to write the Adventures of a Lady Traveller if you keep it up.'

'Alice says there are lots of heavy lady travellers in Ibiza.'

'Heavy ladies?' said Cy. 'Shall I tell you how I know a heavy lady?' I nodded. 'By her smell.'

He rummaged amongst a suitcase of socks and brought out a small bottle of perfume, which he applied to my nose.

'That's what the *real* heavy ladies wear,' he informed me like it was a state secret, 'the rest are kidding themselves with patchouli. Have another smell,' he insisted. 'Don't you find it sexy?' He rubbed some round my ears and then put a dot on the end of his nose and inhaled. 'I keep it around just to get turned on by the smell,' he said.

'Do you think I should get some?' I asked. 'Do I qualify?'

'I wouldn't have told you the secret if I hadn't wanted you to use it,' said Cy. 'You're my favourite freak, and I want you to be a success. Anita Pallenberg wears it,' he added encouragingly.

'Good enough,' I said, 'but don't go telling everybody.'

'You're the chatterbox, not me,' said Cy. The cards all flew in the air as his left-handed version of the one-handed weave shuffle misfired. 'I'm out of practice. Let's go to an afternoon movie.'

'In the daytime?' I queried.

'I never go at night,' he said, 'too many people, too much hustle. Besides, it makes me high to come out in the daylight and see all those office workers.'

'I don't like looking at them,' I said.

'They're the ones you see if you go to the movies at night. And they crackle and whisper and fidget.'

In the cool dark emptiness of the afternoon performance I remembered my childhood film-going and realised it was more convenient never to grow up. Cy directed the movie as it went along, which added an extra dimension of unreality, and when we stepped out into the bright sunlight and rush hour I hardly knew who I was. Cy insisted we went on the underground, which I hadn't entered for two years. I found myself crushed between pastry-faced secretaries in their Oxford Street uniforms who stared at me as though I was a hippy outrage. I looked at the advertisements and saw myself in black-and-white surrounded by a lot of dirty words in day-glo, with Jay hovering ghost-like over my shoulder. I'd just received a postcard of a vase of roses from him saying he was cooling himself out in the countryside and would be in touch. Before I left I wrote to Larry explaining what had happened and telling him I was going to stay with my parents until I felt better. I didn't want to speak to Mason, but left the address of the Ibiza Post Office for Cy to give anyone in an emergency.

'And I'd like you to have this,' I said, handing him something pink.

'What is it?' he asked.

'A butterfly T-shirt,' I said, 'I had three, I gave one to Larry because he was special.'

Cy held up the pink sleeveless vest with a coloured butterfly painted across the front. He tried it on and looked at himself in the mirror.

'You can see a lot of my body,' he said, flexing his muscles. He could have been a road worker.

'Your tan looks good against the pink,' I said.

He stroked the colours of the butterfly wings in the reflection of the mirror.

'Butterfly T-shirt, eh?' he mused. 'Who's going to qualify for the last one? Taking it with you?'

'Just in case,' I said.

'And your heavy lady perfume …'

'And my Marmite …'

'So if I meet two other guys wearing butterfly T-shirts, we'll know who we've got in common.'

'Oh, the butterflies are all different,' I said, 'and you're the only one I'm telling it to this way.'

'So the others will think it's coincidence?' he laughed, 'reckon it'd have to be, and one I'd like to film.'

'So you'll be able to wear it?' I asked.

'Just right for the Cannes Film Festival,' he said, 'now there's a scene …'

'I'm finished with movies,' I said.

'You should finish with that Mason Radar.'

'I will.'

'You've been saying that since I've known you.' He always got irritated when we argued about Mason.

'I've been waiting for the power to fade,' I said.

'What power? Blind Power!' Cy laughed.

'I'm not talking about it at the moment. Anyway, there isn't time.' I could hear my taxi arriving for the airport.

Cy carried my old cracked suitcase outside. Larry had

been wearing a blue T-shirt with a green and orange butterfly across his thin chest when he had driven me to the airport
in the sun. Cy shivered in the cool evening air.

'Sock it to them over there,' he said, 'and don't forget, you
can only belong to *yourself*.' He shook me gently by the
shoulders, stuck a joint in my mouth and winked.

17

'A nice cup of tea, I think,' said Atmos, flashing his torch round the baked earth interior of the white plaster-cast cottage.

'That's a ritual I've been without,' I remarked. 'American tea bags just aren't the same. Cy drinks instant coffee and I squeeze oranges.'

'Re-open memory lane,' called Atmos from a large room that had a corner of camping equipment for basic nutritional needs on the occasional balanced plank. I added my jar of Marmite to the unfamiliar packets and jars. Alice was lighting candles and I could see they hadn't been in residence long enough to glamourize its natural potential beyond foam rubber and a couple of choice hangings.

'What do you think?' asked Alice, sitting at the all-purpose table and arranging three incompatible tea-cups.

'I like it,' I said, 'of course I do.'

'You should see some of the houses that are incredibly together.'

'I can imagine,' I said, 'it's the perfect setting.'

The modern existence of Mandrax Mansions was a uneasy recipient for the expression of our time-jumbled culture, for it had been geometrically designed for Heals and Habitat. This peasant palace had a natural non-symmetry that could only be enhanced by our kind of taste, and needed no camouflage to feel good. It was like playing house with all the freedom of childhood.

'I brought some acid through in my ears,' I told them, 'to have a nature trip on your roof.'

'Atmos brought in a hundred Sunshine strapped to his balls,' said Alice, 'a present to the island from an old freak.'

'The island's loaded,' said Atmos, bringing in the tea, 'with just about anything you could want.'

'So many *freaks*,' said Alice, 'lots of heavy ladies and lots of heavy trips. Atmos found himself out here with thirteen one night.'

'What happened?'

'Half of them split and the rest of us dropped acid and just took it as it came.'

'I couldn't get anything together,' he said, 'all these chicks giggling and carrying on like I wasn't there. Amazing.'

'You loved it,' said Alice fondly. 'He just lay there in his element.'

'I was digging feeling utterly superfluous,' he said. 'There was nothing else I could do.'

'He managed to sneak off with a couple of them,' said Alice. 'I saw you.'

'So you've been busy,' I said.

'Had a lot of clap to clear up first,' he said. 'Chicks kept asking to meet me and I thought I was in luck but all they wanted was Tetracycline.'

'It can be boring,' said Alice, 'listening to vaginal complaints all the time. And then when their cunts are better they start laying other problems on him. They think he can cure their heads as well.'

'I do my best,' Atmos said.

'You mean you fuck them.'

'That's all they need, a hot meat injection.'

'What about me?' queried Alice. 'You can't even get rid of my cough!' She had had a chesty whoop as long as I had known her.

'It's not getting any worse, is it?' demanded Atmos.

'But it's not getting any better either,' she complained. 'I thought the fresh air would help.'

Atmos shone a torch down her throat and asked her what colour her spit was. Then he brought a small phial out of his black bag and measured out some white powder on to the end of her tongue.

'What's that?' I asked.

'Concentrated bracken flower. I'm trying to break away from chemical remedies. The side-effects just can't be good, and we all know illness comes from the mind, don't we?' He patted Alice's knee.

'Do you think I need a hot meat injection too?' she asked.

'I'm sure you do, dear,' he said.

Alice was curious to hear what had happened with Larry, but nodded wisely when I told her I still wasn't sure myself.

'I've come out here to escape those kind of problems,' I said, trying to let them know my state of mind.

'You're safe with us,' said Atmos, 'as long as you want to stay.'

My room had two heavy low-slung beams and a wine press built into the corner, a rickety wooden bed and an orange box. The floor was rough and at first I didn't want to walk without shoes. The mattress felt musty and I wondered if it was alive. I lay under my Moroccan blanket with my sleeping rag and watched the candle making eerie flickers and listening to the night noises through the slit window. When I blew out the light to go to sleep I was almost frightened by the over-whelming blackness that surrounded me. I could hear Radio Monte Carlo from the other bedroom and tried to imagine the house as it used to be.

A shaft of sunlight lit my room in the morning, and I opened my little wooden shutter to let in as much as possible. Atmos was drawing water from the well, which had to be used as sparingly as possible. I remembered the 'pure' water that Larry bought in bright blue plastic cylinders.

'The shit hole is first right at the end of the wall,' he said, 'but it's engaged at the moment.'

Alice came round the wall stark naked with a roll of Andrex in her hand. I took my turn and couldn't resist peeking at all the old turds. There was something rather friendly about losing the ultimate privacy and I squatted down to pretend I'd never felt a plastic seat round my bottom. After a while it didn't bother me and I could just enjoy the view over the valley. There were only two other houses in sight on the colourful countryside, and I could hear sheep bells ringing and distant Spanish voices in fields.

After cornflakes we bumped our way down the hazardous dirt track that led to the main road and I could feel the sea in the air that blew in my face. The beach they used was small and perfect, and although I didn't really want to meet anyone until I had an inconspicuous tan, we were soon surrounded by some of Atmos and Alice's new friends. It seemed as if they knew me already, and after a couple of days I could have been there for months.

When we'd had enough beach we drove to the old town for provisions and meetings. There was something of Central Park on Sunday about the bars around the Old Port, though the crowd of freaks that well out-numbered the natives and straight tourists were the strangest and most exotic I had yet been amongst. My eyes couldn't move fast enough to take in the highest vogue of true freak fashion that moved from table to table. Wildly ornate or starkly simple, everyone made their own charisma through their clothes and presentation. The conversations boggled me as much, for I had no adventures to compare with these intrepid international pilgrims. The guys were stoned-out business men in the black market of pleasure, talking a paranoid code of deals and rip-offs, frayed nerves and freak-outs. And the chicks were more than chicks, working the same business in their own way. Daphne from Texas with hair like Jean Harlow had just finished working as a physiotherapist in New York where she found she could treble her wage by giving head. Pollen Cassidy had just returned from a two-year jail sentence in Turkey and I'd never have guessed the persecution she'd been through. Destiny Jones had been living 12,000 feet above sea level in a magic cave of stalagmites with a group of Afghani tribesmen who had pierced her nose with a golden ring. Germaine Greer should get her bicycle out.

Atmos left Alice and me at the house the next day and I dropped a little acid. I sat on the flat grassy roof with Alice, who soon noticed she was picking up on my high. My secret thoughts had nothing to do with this time and place, but I needed to know hers to feel the way of things on this island. She had found herself drawn via Atmos into a couple of experiences with chicks that had just seemed the easiest thing to do at the time, and not without a sweet kind of pleasure. But she found the situation less interesting without his presence, for her feelings were still mixed enough to need his guidance. She had also had her own personal sexual coups; one nameless random freak had picked her up on the back of his horse, abducted her back to her house, and galloped off into the night after loving her.

'It was very Arthurian,' she said, 'and I also got turned on to a couple of musicians.'

'Who were they?' I asked.

'One was a young cat who played these really moody songs. We just sat and held hands, but that's cool, we didn't need to make it that time. I'll see him again. He knows you.'

'Have I slept with him?'

'I don't think so. He didn't say much. And the other was a huge spade drummer who gave off this incredible power through his drums, and even when he wasn't playing you could feel it.' She sat up and raised her hands in the air and her little tits pointed straight at me. She widened and rolled her eyes and tried to make me feel it. 'I was very high and wanted to submit to him. I followed him outside and when he looked at me I was helpless and could only stare into his dark, dark eyes. He knew and I knew, and I guess we didn't need to know any more. So I went back inside.'

'You're turning into me,' I said.

She paused to work it out. 'I can dig it,' she said slowly. 'I really get off on good music. But you're not turning into me, are you?'

'I can't find anybody to turn into,' I said.

'Maybe you don't have to,' she said, 'but sometimes I feel that I'm losing my identity in Atmos. I was into many more things of my own before I met him; now he seems to be my only thing.'

'He's just given you a different identity,' I suggested.

'But it's part of his, and I want my own. Whenever I go somewhere alone I'm asked "where's Atmos?"'

'The same probably happens to him.'

'I don't know what happens to him half the time,' she said, 'Scorpios are so secretive, he can close up, boom, just like that, and go all icy and detached.'

She clapped her hands in front of her face and stood up. She spun round the roof dancing and waving a pair of knickers over her head.

'Wheeeeee!' she called out over the valley, 'I'm the cosmic go-go dancer! When will I be a star?'

'Always,' I said, and she came over and stroked my hair. I could have done something about it, but played around with words instead. We babbled on about identities until there were no more answers, and all the time I was thinking why don't we just shut up and love each other. But we'd have to talk about it afterwards and re-run it all for Atmos and I still hadn't decided whether that was what I'd come for.

18

'When we need a shower we go to Travers' place,' Atmos told me. 'He's got a proper house the other side of town.'

'Oscar sent him a chick once,' I remembered, 'and wrote about him in his book. 'What is he?'

'You'll like him,' Alice said, 'he's got some good stories.'

'He's an International Situational Manipulator,' said Atmos.

'Like all the guys here,' said Alice, 'only he's been at it longer.'

'I don't see why I should like him at all,' I said. 'I don't want to be manipulated.'

'Yes you do,' said Atmos, 'you're dying for it.'

'You'll like him,' insisted Alice. 'He'll make you laugh.'

'That's all right then,' I said, to apologise for my defensiveness.

It was evening when we drove to Travers' place, which was far more central. The house had tiled flooring and electricity and had been lived in for some time. There was a sleepy-eyed chick called Dormadina staying there who said Travers was out visiting. We took our showers and sat around while she stumbled out her problems to Atmos, who couldn't have helped even if she'd been able to listen. Before we left the bead curtains rattled dramatically and an extremely exotic figure stepped into the centre of attention. She was very tanned and dressed in leather slave-gear, sandals laced up to her thighs and lots of chains that jingled commandingly. She stood imperiously just inside the door and looked at us.

'Hi, Spangle,' murmured Dormadina to herself.

But Spangle's eyes were concentrating on Atmos and Alice and I could feel a heavy triangle in the air.

'Hello,' said Alice feebly.

Atmos went over to her and kissed her lightly on the cheek. The he drew her towards me.

'Spangle, this is Tiptree,' he said with courtesy.

'Tiptree, Spangle.'

She nodded at me then stared at him challengingly.

'Well, what's happening?' she demanded.

'You look great,' said Atmos, giving her a look of appreciation.

'Actually, we're just off,' asserted Alice. 'We came to see Travers.'

Spangle flashed her eyes at Alice's briefly. Then she turned back to Atmos.

'So nothing's happening,' she said. 'How about a lift into town?'

The conversation was artificially light until we dropped her outside the health restaurant. Bumping our way back to the house Alice gave me her version of the night with Spangle. Atmos drove silently, and my attention was mesmerized by his manipulation of the road. There was a note pinned to the door of the house.

'It's from Travers,' said Alice, squinting at the writing with the torch. 'He came to visit and …' she paused to decipher the message '… and he wants us to go on a yacht tomorrow with someone called Great Dan.'

'Maybe that's the name of the boat,' suggested Atmos.

There was a lot of hanging around the next day before we finally stepped off land and Travers still hadn't arrived. Great Dan was a minor millionaire of large proportions who fancied a bit of freak company. There were quite a few of us already on board, and he was impatient to leave. I felt disappointed at missing Travers again until Atmos shouted 'Here he comes' and I saw two figures hastily approaching the boat. I recognised Spangle, and I wondered if somehow she was his lady. She didn't look quite as stunning today and smiling past her I saw Travers. I hadn't expected him to have a beard, but his eyes twinkled blue and his hennaed hair glowed like a halo round his head. He swayed his lean body across the gang-plank, laughing at the excitement of it all and nearly dropping the basket from his shoulder. He was breathless and amazed at catching us still there and looked around the cabin eagerly to see who we were. Atmos introduced me, and as we reached to shake hands the boat rolled and we missed each other.

'We missed each other last night as well,' he said, laughing and losing his balance as the boat rolled again. 'What's going on? I think I'd better sit down.'

'Ahoy down there!' shouted Great Dan from the cockpit. 'We're away now.'

The boat had started to pitch and we could feel the rhythm of the sea increase. Travers laughed enthusiastically and I giggled nervously.

'How about passing one of those joints that I don't seem to be getting?' called down Great Dan, putting on a pair of headphones and turning up a wild rock tape full volume. He dragged on the offered joint with a frenetic urgency to get high, going red around the neck and starting to perspire at the end of his nose. Gradually his whole face was glowing, and he seemed to slobber with delight as he felt the madness enter his mind. He jerked recklessly on the tiller with nautical exhilaration and I was sure the boat was going to turn over. We could hardly keep our seats, things were crashing down around us and I was feeling stranger than high. 'I think it's time to move,' said Travers, and so did everyone else. We clumsily manoeuvred our way out of the small crowded cabin to find ourselves completely surrounded by choppy blue sea and brisk salty air. I found myself a rope to hang on to, though it was impossible to remain in a comfortable position. I could see Travers making his way round all the people now on the deck and hoped my wits would revive by the time he got to me. Through my giddiness I could feel anticipation at his approach, but tried not to recognise it.

'So, Miss Gibbon,' he said, when he finally crawled towards me over the top of a lifeboat with spray sparkling in his beard. 'What's it like to have balled all those pop musicians and lived to tell the tale?'

'Pretty exhausting,' I said, 'I've had to take a holiday.'

'What made you come to this crazy island?' he asked.

'My friends are here,' I said, looking in their direction.

'They told me about you,' he said.

It felt like a set-up, but the boat was lurching too much for me to care.

'And I came for some rest,' I complained, 'this isn't much good. Where are all the naked bodies on the poop?'

'They'll be there,' he said, 'anyway, what's made you so tired?'

'Guys,' I said, rather aggressively.

'You look fine to me,' he said, 'and here comes the sun. It's never far away.'

It wasn't hot enough to relax in, but we anchored somewhere not so rough and some hardy bodies jumped into the clear blue sea. When we turned back to port and the boat started lurching again Travers found himself a seat at the top of the cabin steps, put a cushion between his legs on the floor, and asked me if I'd like to sit down. It was the ideal compromise. I was seated comfortably out of the wind, yet could take in the necessary air and view to contain my giddiness. I gave a passing thought to Spangle, who had remained in the cabin with her knitting, and as people clambered down again to relax, she put away her needles and balls and went up on deck.

'Hey Spangle,' murmured Travers, as she passed us.

'Hey you two,' she grinned at us, and I couldn't feel anything more than friendship between them.

'Spangle rents part of my house,' Travers explained. 'You two would have some stories to exchange.'

Atmos and Alice had noticed where I was sitting, and I stared down at Travers' feet. They were gnarled brown and strapped into stout Christ-like sandals. I could only find them attractive by thinking they were holy. I closed my eyes and let my body touch his leg. Then I felt his fingers in my hair, on my neck and trailing down my arms. When I closed my eyes I could still feel the dizziness more than I could feel him, but gradually the two became the same and I felt myself in a high sensual fantasy. I turned to look at him and saw a gentle friend that I could do with. He smiled down at me and said hey, and then we could both sense each other. I thought about bunks and reckoned Great Dan would have a large one somewhere, and noticed at the same time that Atmos and Alice weren't in the cabin and hadn't gone on deck either.

'You pinched my boat fantasy,' I told Alice later, when we were back in town eating ice-creams. 'I wanted to compare it with the train incident.'

'And the aeroplane attempt,' she said, 'well, the ceiling was too low and the bed was covered with life jackets.'

'But what about the movement?' I asked.

'Couldn't,' said Atmos.

The evening was taking its direction and Travers was still beside me, nothing stated. Atmos and Alice started to get into a heavy discussion about Plans and Freedom and moved to the other end of the table.

'I have to go to Mad Mario's house,' Travers told me. 'Do you want to come?'

'I don't know,' I said, and looked to the other end of the table. They were far away and I felt alone.

'You don't have to decide yet,' said Travers, 'I'm going to find a lift and I'll pass by this way.'

I nodded and watched him jaunt off with his basket, stopping here and there to speak before disappearing round a corner. Atmos and Alice were trying to work out some situation, and I wished they would make up their minds so that I could make up mine. Unless they would come with me, going with Travers into the night meant more than a giddy fantasy on a boat. But they had other pursuits, and Atmos stood up.

'I'm off,' he said, 'I'm leaving the car with Alice.'

We sat silent while he walked away. Alice sighed.

'I'm going to hang out here for a bit,' she said, 'I suppose you're going with Travers.'

'I suppose I am,' I said.

She stared at me for a while. 'I'm going to talk to Frisby,' she said, and got up to join another table.

I felt almost deserted, and by the time Travers appeared I was glad to see him. He clambered out of an old car and came over to my lonely table.

'Well, Gibbon, how do you feel?' he asked, 'want to take a ride?'

'How will I get home?' I feebly felt obliged to ask. 'I've no idea even where I live.'

'That's easy,' he said. 'Something will work out. Or you can stay with me. That's easy too.' He saw me catch my lip. 'I won't do anything you don't want,' he added, 'I like your company.'

'Then it's all easy,' I said, standing up. I seemed to have made some kind of decision, and felt much better.

19

The open car was crowded with the usual freaks and we bounced and wound our way between little walls up the dark countryside. Sitting on Travers' knee with the sweet-smelling air in my face I wondered about his Rip Van Winkle beard. Too bohemian for the town-time person I used to be, the dangerous appeal of a two-week growth had been the most I could find attractive before. But now, who was I, and to answer myself I only had to turn my head and my face was up to his. Too close to stop, our mouths met, and I could taste the sea and feel the grass and smell the whole countryside in his face.

We finally parked in a little clearing half-way up a rubble track and climbed over a couple of broken-down walls towards the flickering candle-lit windows. Another plaster-cast cottage full of living freaks on mattresses, smoking endless water-pipes and getting far too high. After half-an-hour of solid smoking the strongest drug I'd ever known, the guy who had driven us stumbled out of the door and I wondered how we'd get back.

'He's having the horrors,' said someone from the door-way with a torch. 'Now he's vomiting… he's still having the horrors… he's vomiting again… he'll be all right …'

I wondered what on earth we could be smoking because I couldn't feel my body and didn't know what to do with my mind. Travers told me it was home-made Grade I with datura. I was already wasted by the day, and now I was miles away from anywhere and so high I was frightened. I could feel a paranoia creeping through my brain that I didn't recognise and tried to analyze. There were too many chicks in the room with a well-travelled self-confidence who all seemed very intimate with Travers, and I felt like a lamb for the slaughter under their scrutiny and high sexual vibes. The tapes of wailing monks in a Marrakesh market place droned on and on until I wondered how anyone else could stand it… and the pipes kept coming faster and faster until I passed… for the first time in ages, I shook my head, I couldn't get any higher.

'Give yourself a break, baby,' said the chick sitting next to me, after I'd passed three times.

My head exploded with resentment at being treated like a baby-straight and I dive-bombed my mind on to a different level where I could do anything if I had to. I didn't refuse another pipe and fidgeted my body to keep the numbness from creeping into a black-out. Owning up to myself that I was completely zonked kept me in some kind of perspective, and I could see that most of the others were horizontal by now. I wanted to do the same but couldn't allow it, and the pipes kept coming, followed by some sweet mint tea and more pipes. Too much was the password on this island, and I wondered whether I could take it.

The driver of the car claimed to have recovered, and we tried to identify our baskets from the pile in the corner. The night was black outside and we walked into a disused well before we located the car.

'I want to drive,' said a chick carrying two basket. 'Mel's too freaked out.'

'I heard that,' said Mel, starting the car roughly. 'And I'm quite all right.'

'There's a lot of people in this car,' she told him, as we careered forwards just missing a looming tree.

'Are you trying to give me the horrors?' he demanded, wrenching on the steering wheel.

'I'm just worried about people's lives,' she emphasised, and he clenched his jaw and accelerated.

We all sat grimly hypnotised by the road as Mel scraped his way relentlessly downwards. It seemed endless, and then we were going up again towards Travers' house. Outside the door we warmly congratulated Mel and weakly tottered inside. Now there was space in my mind for the final drama of the long day into night. I deliciously tortured myself with guilt remembering Larry and all those promises on my conscience.

'Let's just get into bed,' said Travers, 'I'm too spaced to think of anything else.'

I wondered if he was too spaced to make love, and I sat shyly on the edge of the thin foam between us and the hard boards of the bed. I forgot about Larry and waited for Travers.

'Hey Gibbon,' he said softly, and I looked at him anxiously. 'What are you waiting for?' he asked, and reached out his arms for me.

'I just felt foolish for a moment,' I told him, and lay down in his arms.

'Why's that?' he asked, stroking my back.

'Because I haven't slept with anyone for so long and the last time was too heavy and I've been confused since then about all this,' I blurted out, wanting to explain everything.

'I'll be gentle,' he said, and he was more than that, it was so nice to be loving someone again and loving them so well. I thought I'd forgotten how and knew I would be eternally grateful to the man on the island who brought it all back to me. Travers said he wanted more of me and my funky body and asked me to come and stay.

'I like being with you,' he said, 'and however you want to be with me that's fine.'

So it was easy to say yes, though I was sorry to leave the house on the hill.

'I'd like to come back sometime,' I said to Atmos, 'and I still want to drop a lot of acid on your roof.'

'I'm happy you're with Travers,' Atmos told me. 'I knew it was going to happen even before you got here.'

'Why didn't you tell me?' I asked.

'Because no one can tell you anything,' said Atmos, 'without you thinking you're under some kind of pressure. So I kept quiet and let it happen.'

'Are you beginning to understand me?' I demanded. 'Is that why you haven't tried to touch me since I arrived?'

'There are other ladies, you know,' Atmos reminded me.

'I know that,' I said impatiently, 'but for me, anticipation is as big a buzz as gratification.'

'Well, it looks like it's anticipation I'll have to be satisfied with for the moment,' he said.

'Only with me,' I replied, 'the others are falling all over you. I'm glad I'm not Alice.'

'Poor Alice,' he said, 'she's confused again. She thinks she wants to have a baby.'

'That's not a good idea, is it?' I asked.

'Haven't we all got enough problems?' he answered.

Alice was in the orchard picking flowers. She was sad that I was moving, but glad that I'd found Travers.

'I'm coming back and we'll all trip out together,' I told her.

'I've taken too many trips on this island,' she said. 'Sometimes I wonder where it's all taking me.'

'Atmos tells me you're talking about babies,' I said.

'Well, I feel I've been with him long enough to have something to show for it,' she said. 'It's time for certain things to be fulfilled. It says so in my chart.'

'What does Atmos say?' I asked.

'What you'd expect,' she said a little bitterly. 'Anything I do is my own responsibility. He won't actually stop me, but that's not enough, is it?'

'No,' I said, 'maybe if you wait he'll change his mind.'

'He says he won't and then it might be too late for me,' she said. 'I thought if I couldn't be a movie star I might at least be a mother.'

'You haven't been a movie star yet,' I said.

'I know,' she said gloomily, 'there isn't enough time.'

I left her pondering in the orchard to re-enter my relationship with Travers. We played around with each other all the time, touching and responding constantly, hardly ever out of each other's company. We cruised around the town at night and slept well into the day. Travers took a lot of siestas as well, so I sweated myself a tan on the roof. I wasn't getting to the beach as much as planned, life was even too lazy for that, but I did a lot of walking up and down the dry stony hillside. I wondered whether I should make a domestic demonstration, but Dormadina made the occasional effort in return for her refuge in the spare room, so I limited myself to making the bed.

Travers gave me the stories that were like a picture book and jig-saw puzzle to his life. He'd lived the American dream to disprove it and found himself breaking rocks in a Turkish prison to disprove it further. He'd travelled round the world with nomads in the desert, tribesmen in the hills; galloping Kurds in Kurdistan, riots in Eastern states, stop-offs in Tibetan monasteries and Indian temples, he'd roamed through different cultures to find his own.

'I pressed my ear to the Arabian Desert,' he told me, 'and I could hear the Bedouins galloping up to a thousand miles away in the sand. Unless it was the oil wells pumping,' he added ruefully.

'Oh no, it was the night riders,' I said, convinced of the images behind my eyes.

He'd met crazy people and done crazy things just to keep alive, and his emotional journey had evolved through the turmoil. He'd been married three times, twice to the same chick, who had loved him so much he could have done anything with her. But she had brought out bad things in him, for some reason he couldn't explain in words, and he hated himself when he was with her. He used to leave her alone most of the time while he fucked around with other chicks, and she'd wait and go on waiting, and wouldn't let anyone else touch her. He hardly touched her either, because he knew that if he explored her sexually she would get such a hold on him that he'd be lost, and the terror of what that would turn him into scared him. So they tortured each other from a distance; even marrying someone else inbetween couldn't break the cruel love. The other marriage had been to a rich lady so hung up on chicks that Travers was the only man who could please her. She gave him her chicks, he gave her his, and in nine months he learnt all he ever needed to know about ladies. Apart from his first wife; he was drawn back to her again but it didn't get any better and she got so spaced out in the relationship that she ran off with a junkie genius writer who depended on her like a child and who couldn't even make love.

'I've always know junkies and I guess I always will,' he said, 'I've always been stoned and forgotten what it's like to be straight.'

Even in the freezing junkie prison he found himself in out East, acid was smuggled into him. Sitting in the snow out of his brain he'd seen a line from an Ezra Pound poem that had given him some hope. He examined himself closely during the several years he was in gaol and turned his head around emotionally.

His wife had put her junkie in some sort of shape and the first thing he wrote again was a political piece to try and get Travers out of gaol.

'She made him,' Travers told me, 'even though he knew that if I got released and if I sent for her she'd go. But I never sent for her again.'

He had rejected that kind of relationship for ever. He was

scared to dig up the past where love was obsessive and full of hooks. He wanted to love without the pain of jealousy and possession. Each relationship could now occupy its own place in his memory, being neither better no worse than any other, just special in its own way. He could promise love and friendship without conditions, a time and a place, but not for ever. I saw his logic and I saw my relationship in perspective with countless others.

'I've told you all about myself so soon,' he said. 'I haven't done this before. How do you feel about me now?'

'Your head seems pretty far on,' I told him, 'it's where I'd like to be, it's the way I'm looking for.'

I had told him most of my stories too, and now we found ourselves mind to mind in that state that previously transcended sex for me. Like with Jay, like with Atmos, like with Cy. There were mental barriers with guys I gave myself to physically and vice versa. If I could reconcile this through Travers I would have made a breakthrough. I stared at him. Now that I knew his mind did I still want his body? He could read my thoughts.

'Well, Gibbon?' he asked. 'Can I still play with you?'

'You've given me choice,' I said. 'And you've given me the rules.'

'No rules,' he said, 'plenty of choice.'

'That's how it should be, shouldn't it?' I asked.

'Of course,' he said, 'though it isn't always easy.'

'I'll play,' I said. It sounded easier than Larry's game.

20

We waited in the gentle early evening. A sweat broke out on my forehead and a coldness tingled under my skin, then the warmth spread through my body, loosening it to the metabolic magic. The landscape deepened in dimension and the sun spread golden into the purple clouds. Murmurs from the fields wafted over me and sheep bells rang in my temples. I focused one last look at my friends before I was taken and time was lost. It was the ultimate high, this chemical love-trip on the roof, and there were no words as the changes from day into night spread slowly over us. Did the crickets tick for ever, and when did the stars start to sparkle, I asked myself, myself, who was I? How cold it was inside my body as consciousness returned to my ego. I am Tiptree Gibbon and there is Alice my sister in front of me. I could see her so clearly I didn't have to look. Atmos should be somewhere, but I couldn't feel him, and then I knew he was behind me. For Travers was beside me now, and I turned to remember him. He was a dark shadow that I could touch, and I peered into him. I smiled at him, and he recognised me. Contact flowed between us and we were joined.

'Hey Gibbon,' he whispered, 'I can feel your spirit, I can feel your unconscious.'

'What's it like?' I asked.

'It feels good,' he said, 'and I wonder at you for showing it to me.'

'It wants to be inside you,' I said, 'to feel your love.'

'It's yours,' he said.

'Through you I can love everything,' I said. The love vibes were running riot inside me.

'I can hear you,' said Alice. 'Have we come back? Where's Atmos?'

'Somewhere here,' said Atmos weakly from a dark corner. 'But I don't know where.'

Now we could hear ourselves and memory filtered back. I moved clumsily and tried again.

'I have to move,' I said. 'I think I'm cold.'

But I didn't know which way I was facing and had to feel my way round the little wall to find the steps to earth. Travers fumbled after me, and unsteadily we clambered down with rubbery limbs. It was a different world on the ground, to feel the living earth beneath me led me away from the house into the blackness, where I crouched in some long grass and watched the little house flicker into life.

Back inside the house I saw my friends' faces weak with shock. Travers was abandoned on a mattress and Alice was trying to look for something.

'Have you got the sleeping bag?' she asked me.

'I don't know,' I said. 'I think Travers brought it down.'

'I don't remember,' said Travers helplessly.

'I want to lie on the roof in the sleeping bag and look at the cosmos,' said Alice, 'but I can't find it.'

'Travers ate it,' I said.

Everyone laughed hysterically.

'It's still on the roof, dear,' said Atmos, concentrating very hard on sticking three skins together. Alice stared at him intently then went outside.

'I've forgotten how to roll,' said Atmos from the table. I tried to cut a slice of bread and couldn't co-ordinate. I ate a packet of crisps instead.

'It's not there,' said Alice, appearing again.

'The sky?' asked Atmos.

'The sleeping bag,' said Alice crossly. 'I don't understand it.'

'I told you, Travers ate it,' I said.

Travers looked at me and giggled.

'Are you sure?' he asked me, 'I don't remember.'

'Of course you don't' I said.

Nobody was quite sure by now, and Alice sighed in despair. She sat and fiddled for Radio Geronimo on the radio. Suddenly Spooky Tooth blared out with a heavy rock number that sounded ludicrous coming out of such a small box in the middle of nowhere.

'Maybe I'm amazed,' sang Paul McCartney next, 'at the way you love me all the time,' and I was a million miles away with Larry. At the end of the record Alice straightened herself.

'He's found it,' she announced.

'What's he found?' asked Atmos.

'The woman behind the man,' she stated.

Atmos and Travers appeared bewildered. She looked at them, waiting for them to understand, and then started tying herself in verbal knots trying to explain.

'I understand,' I interrupted her. Atmos and Travers looked at me questioningly. 'Don't worry about it,' I told them, 'it's chickshit.'

We didn't quite know what to do with ourselves, and stumbled around mentally and physically, feeling claustrophobic inside, but lost out in the darkness. I found Atmos playing with a flashlight in the front yard, clicking it on and off to illuminate things like an antiquated slide projector. He sat cross-legged and blinked the light up at himself from the ground, shining like a sinister sphinx. We sat in a row like at the movies and shrieked with delight at every new image. Then my thoughts started to wander, and I felt something primitive within me. I wanted to go into the fields for something, then a fantasy of being fucked in a lush green meadow came to me. I looked for Travers.

'Let's go out there,' I said to him, and pulled him by the hand. I threw my knickers over the gate as we felt our way over the rough land. It was like walking on the moon; the eerie night light made everything unfamiliar and hazardous. There was no direction and no lush green meadow, only long spiky grass and kinetic Spanish trees. I went down on my hands and knees under one of the trees to see if the ground was soft.

'Where are you, Gibbon?' asked Travers, finding himself standing alone. 'What are you doing down there?'

'I had a fantasy about being fucked in a lush green meadow,' I told him.

He laughed, and knelt down beside me.

'You're crazy,' he said, and laughed again, 'but it's a lovely fantasy. I wouldn't know where to start, my mind's too far out of my body.'

'It doesn't matter,' I said, and stood up, 'the ground's too rough. And I'm cold without my knickers.'

He felt my bare bottom under my white Indian shirt.

'I took them off for the occasion,' I told him.

He held me close and said he loved me.

'And I've got to have a pee,' he said.

I stood beside him while he undid his trousers. I took him in my hands and felt the hot water passing through. I entered his body and felt it for myself, the whole sensation he was having. I stood motionless beside him while he finished with a gasp.

'What are you doing?' he asked breathlessly, 'you're taking me right over.'

'It was a substitute for the lush green meadow,' I told him, and laughing, we somehow found our way back to the house. We were tired, but couldn't stop the chemical charging round in our heads. I relaxed my body and enjoyed my thoughts. Suddenly Alice grabbed the radio and made her way up the low steps to the bedroom she shared with Atmos. We watched her with vague surprise.

'Why doesn't everyone come up here?' she paused outside the doorway. 'It's comfier up here.' Then she disappeared and we listened to the faintness of the radio. I looked at Travers and Atmos. They were looking at each other and didn't move.

'I think we're all right down here, dear,' called Atmos.

Alice re-appeared, guilty and waif-like.

'I have to lie down,' she said. 'Why don't we all lie down together?'

'Because we're down here,' said Atmos.

Their roles seemed to have got reversed in some way, Alice's initiative had taken me by surprise, and Atmos was unusually negative. Travers could giggle through any drama, and I made no comment while I chided myself with indecision. Alice had gone back into the bedroom and nobody moved. I wanted to break the awkward silence.

'I'm going to see Alice,' I said, and felt four eyes following me. I stepped into the bedroom and saw Alice lying on the large mattress, the candles flickering light on to the green shawl that hung like a canopy from the low ceiling. We stared at each other, then she reached out her arms towards me. I knelt in front of her on the edge of the bed, and we put our arms around each other. Then we looked long into each other's faces and I just let my feeling for her come out of my eyes and fall all around her. She seemed transfixed, and I wanted to kiss her. Her mouth was small and soft, and her tongue just darted in and out a fraction to touch mine. As we withdrew I saw a blond-haired choirboy with the softest features and the gentlest smile (and I wondered). We lay beside each other waiting and giggling. Atmos stood tall in the doorway.

'Where's Travers?' I asked.

'He's coming,' said Atmos, and approached the bed.

Travers fell into the room laughing with delight.

We now lay naked in the bed and there was much good-will in the air. I kissed with Travers to heighten my love, then I moved towards Atmos. We paused to catch each other's eyes, and the barriers dissolved, all our games and tactics seemed so petty in the past. His kissing became more urgent and I realised Atmos was going to get right in there while he could. Might as well, I thought, and wondered what Travers was doing to Alice. Atmos stopped his movements and looked down at me.

'I'm losing you,' he said, 'you're not concentrating.'

I stopped my body and closed my eyes. When I looked up again my mind was suitably blank and receptive for his plea-sure. He was as skilful as he should have been and I was just starting to forget who we were and enjoy myself when I felt something hard and cold being slipped into my bum. My memory connected and I froze. I could never take vibrators seriously; they always struck me as totally out of sexual context and even when alone the buzz of the batteries confused my concentration. Still pretty tight-arsed about bum-fucking, I tensed my bottom, hoping he would notice my displeasure. I couldn't believe he was going to attempt a double insertion act, and when it started humming and shaking it was all too silly for words, but I had to say some-thing to stop him.

'No,' I whispered, and pulled away from him. 'Not that.'

'Oh, those repressions,' he said fondly, and poised over me smiling.

'Whose repressions?' I heard Alice call in a muffled voice.

'Mine, I said. 'Please don't worry.'

Atmos had disposed of the vibrator bound to be made in Japan and applied his mouth to my snatch. His tongue was very long and could move very fast, and he soon had my clitoris standing out like an indoor firework. I wanted to give in but didn't because the pleasure of holding off the orgasm had captured my sensations. But then I let myself go into the danger zone just too far, and couldn't get back, for now I didn't want to, and I opened up towards him and pushed down into his face for those last few seconds before I sank back to let the convulsions subside. When I came back to myself he was stroking me and murmuring nonsenses, and I stroked his hair gratefully before I turned my head to see if anyone else was within kissing distance, and there was Alice beside me, with Travers on top of her.

'Hey Gibbon,' he panted, moving in and out of her, 'how are you doing?'

I grinned and stroked Alice's tiny tits that hardly existed when she lay on her back. I kissed with Travers while she ran her fingers through my hair. Atmos came up damp from my snatch to kiss Alice, and I moved to caress her body and finger her baby clit. Then the two guys just stroked us while I made love to Alice, who squealed faintly as I worked my tongue around and inside between her legs, already hot from Travers' attentions. All the tastes were mixed as we permutated in rotation. And in the end who would have the final come and did it have to be all at once? The bodies never seemed to end until there was a final heaving and thrusting in all directions, and it had to be the last time. My head was down amongst the feet, and by then I only knew what was happening by observing the various toes spreading and pushing into the mattress, going rigid and then falling limp like dead fishes. I felt saturated with love and wanted nothing more than some other kind of oblivion. Without looking back or speaking I eased myself from the sticky bodies and crawled out of the door. My rickety bed was still made up and I got in with my sleeping rag and a packet of crisps.

21

Travers was lying beside me and the sun was bright. The -sheets were full of broken crisps; Travers had squashed the half-eaten bag when he'd come to join me in bed. Atmos and Alice were still asleep, but Travers was impatient to get into town to see if some money had arrived for him. I had no desire to hitch a lift or to queue at the Poste Restante on that off-chance that took us there every other day. I told him I'd find him later and watched him jaunt off down the hill. I pottered round eating some of the goodies that we'd brought for last night but hadn't needed. I tidied here and there, and found the sleeping bag hanging from a tree. I sat on the roof waiting for the others to wake and tried to re-capture last night's dream. Although I could remember everything my mind felt blank and disconnected from all that emotion. When I heard movement within the house I went down to join Atmos and Alice in a bowl of cereal. The glow returned somewhat as we giggled over our mad memories, but I felt a different person from the one I was talking about, and Alice wasn't a choir-boy any longer. When the afternoon sun got too hot I went inside and lay staring at the restful lumpy white walls. Atmos came and lay beside me and I couldn't find any reasonable reason why I should mind. He kissed me gently and I responded with a smile.

'I feel I really know you now,' he said.

'More of me,' I said.

'Just watching your face go all soft while I fucked you,' he said, 'told me.'

'Told you what?'

'A lot,' he said. 'Changes you don't know in yourself. It was nice.'

'Yes, it was,' I agreed.

'I enjoy the way you make love,' he told me. 'You respond well.'

'Sometimes I feel terribly feeble,' I said. 'I lose my strength.'

'Well, you're certainly not passive,' said Atmos, 'and that's what I like. Alice is like a child in bed and expects me to do everything. I need more than that, even though I do love her.'

'I'm like that sometimes,' I said.

'Of course you are,' he said, 'but not all the time.'

He had started to fondle my breasts through my thin shirt.

'I am at the moment,' I said, 'after last night.'

'You're not really,' he said, 'you're playing that same old game.'

I felt sad and mean-spirited after all we'd been through and touched his face softly.

'I'm not really,' I said. I laughed. 'I'm not really anything, am I?'

'Yes you are,' he said, 'if you'd let yourself.'

Alice came in to find us half-way into each other.

'Hallo,' she said loudly.

We stayed as we were and smiled at her without guilt.

'Hallo,' I said.

'Can I come in?' she asked.

'Of course,' said Atmos.

She sat on the bed with us, but there wasn't much room for her to join in. I could feel her discomfort and it added to my own confusion. I couldn't help her, Atmos had to play it his way. He didn't ignore her, but he didn't fuck her either, and I started to feel awkward in the unbalanced situation.

Suddenly she stood up and stared at us. Then she ran to the door.

'Alice …' called Atmos.

'I'm not freaking out,' she cried, disappearing. 'I'm not, I'm not …' we heard her crying as she ran to her bedroom. Everything stopped dead. What had happened to last night? Ideals didn't seem to be the same in reality.

'That's that,' I said flatly.

'She's just being silly,' Atmos re-assured me. 'It's bound to be difficult in the beginning.'

'But I understand her,' I said, 'and she didn't have to be silly with me. Doesn't she know that?'

'She'll be all right,' said Atmos.

'I didn't want this to happen,' I said, 'that's why I've waited so long, so we could all understand.'

'She wants to understand,' he said, 'but she's frightened.'

'She wasn't frightened last night,' I said. 'I thought she wanted all this.'

'*I* do,' said Atmos.

But now I didn't know who wanted what, except another unworkable principle. I wanted to give up, but first had to state my case to Alice. Sitting on the bed where we'd loved last night we had very little to say.

'I'm sorry,' she said, 'I thought it would be different with you. I thought I wouldn't mind.'

'You shouldn't,' I said, 'it makes it hard for me if you mind.'

'I know,' she said, 'I know how it should be. I just can't apply it.'

'It should be easier to apply it with me,' I said. 'You know I don't want to spoil anything.'

'I know,' she said again. 'I'm sorry.'

She turned her wide eyes full on me, brimming with tears. I felt cold inside at our sorrow. Atmos came in to save us.

'Too much hilarity,' he said, 'is bound to end in tears.'

We all laughed weakly.

Travers thought it had all been wonderful and I let him keep his illusions. I felt I had none left, even about him, though couldn't admit it, for what would he be to me without my illusion of him? He told me himself for he thought it was what I wanted to hear. He started complaining that he had been on the island too long and felt like an abused playground. It was time for something more restful, something slower, for he was weary of being a continual holiday romance. And it was time to move on with a friend – someone like me perhaps? Yes, we'd move on. He would show me all those places I'd heard so much about and never been to. It was comfortable with him and I could be myself. Nice and easy. I knew I would have to go back to London first, and he was still waiting for the magic money order. If it hadn't arrived within the month I would return to London alone, and either wait for him, meet him somewhere, or come back to Ibiza. I really didn't want to leave without him, because I was scared of getting sucked back into the Mason/Jay problem without anyone to turn to. I refused to contemplate any kind of solution except to pick up some royalties and escape.

Time passed and so did our money, and we both knew something had to be done. Travers started plotting all kinds of schemes and informed me how careful he had to be in his position.

'They're watching me all the time, you know,' he said, one night while we were walking through the old town.

'Who?' I asked.

'CIA, FBI, Interpol, they all know who I am,' he said.

'But they don't mind, do they?' I asked anxiously.

'Of course they do,' he said, 'I'm a political refugee. But there's nothing they can do about it because I know too much.'

'Then you're safe,' I said.

'That doesn't mean I don't have to be careful,' he said.

He quickened his pace and looked round impatiently as I fell behind.

'Why aren't you wearing shoes?' he demanded. 'Do you want to get stopped by the fuzz?'

'For not wearing shoes?' I asked incredulously. Nudity on the beach was one thing, but bare feet were hardly promiscuous.

'They'll use anything they can think of.'

He waited impatiently as I struggled into my cactus sandals.

'Did you see that guy come round the corner behind us?' he asked. I looked round but there were all kinds of people milling around.

'Don't look round,' he said. 'He won't be there now.'

'Do they know that you know?' I asked, as we scurried along.

'I should hope so,' he said. 'If they blow it I'm going to fly over New York in an airship and bomb the Statue of Liberty.'

'Not if you're locked up.'

'They won't do that again. I've got too many people on my side and political martyrs can be embarrassing.'

We reach La Tiera night bar and sat in a dark corner. I wasn't surprised at any type of person that Travers knew, and didn't think twice about the two guys in touristy-type clothes who greeted him. Lots of freaks dress straight to be anonymous at the right moment, and I presumed these were a couple of dealers. Only one of them spoke, and not in English. Whatever it was, Travers spoke it too, and when they left they bowed to me politely.

'And who do you think they were?' Travers asked triumphantly.

'Friends?' I ventured.

He laughed scornfully.

'Didn't you recognise the language? They were from the Greek Drugs Squad.'

'What did they want?' I asked.

'Just checking,' he said, 'just letting me know they knew I was here.'

He seemed to be enjoying it all in a disturbed kind of way, but I found it all extremely surreal. The gentle, carefree Travers had the dangerous glint of a hunted man. Was he so dangerous? Or were they? This was a side of him I'd lightly assumed without realising. He'd been in prison, more than once. He was what my parents called a criminal. Madmen and criminals. If only they knew, what would they think? Myself, I though nothing, I could only feel a detachment that had something to do with sorrow. I was sad because again I didn't know anything more than confusion and didn't like the world at all. And I knew there was something I had missed, some trick of vision, and I knew I had to find it. If nobody else's vision was quite satisfactory, I'd have to invent one of my own. I needed to be alone again to do some research on my mind. The hustle and bustle of travel would be too distracting for me to understand anything, and I'd probably get lost externally as well as internally. I needed my spot, my own cocoon with books and music and a soft bed and my sleeping rag. Travers would find me when he was ready and maybe I'd go with him somewhere. He understood so easily and I loved him for it.

'I'm just running away for a while,' I told him.

'No blame,' he said, 'I'll play with you again, won't I?'

'Of course,' I said.

I gave him my last butterfly T-shirt.

'What a pretty moth,' he said.

'Mothballs,' I laughed, and flew away.

New titles from The Do-Not Press:

Ken Bruen: A WHITE ARREST Bloodlines
1 899344 41 1 – B-format paperback original, £6.50

Galway-born Ken Bruen's most accomplished and darkest crime noir novel to date is a police-procedural, but this is no well-ordered 57th Precinct romp. Centred around the corrupt and seedy worlds of Detective Sergeant Brandt and Chief Inspector Roberts, A White Arrest concerns itself with the search for The Umpire, a cricket-obsessed serial killer that is wiping out the England team. And to add insult to injury a group of vigilantes appear to to doing the police's job for them by stringing up drug-dealers... and the police like it even less than the victims. This first novel in an original and thought provoking new series from the author of whom Books in Ireland said: "If Martin Amis was writing crime novels, this is what he would hope to write."

Mark Sanderson: AUDACIOUS PERVERSION Bloodlines
1 899344 32 2 – B-format paperback original, £6.50

Martin Rudrum, good-looking, young media-mover, has a massive chip on his shoulder. A chip so large it leads him to commit a series of murders in which the medium very much becomes the message. A fast-moving and intelligent thriller, described by one leading Channel 4 TV producer as "Barbara Pym meets Bret Easton Ellis".

Jerry Sykes (ed): MEAN TIME Bloodlines
1 899344 40 3 – B-format paperback original, £6.50

Sixteen original and thought-provoking stories for the Millennium from some of the finest crime writers from USA and Britain, including **Ian Rankin** (current holder of the Crime Writers' Association Gold Dagger for Best Novel) **Ed Gorman, John Harvey, Lauren Henderson, Colin Bateman, Nicholas Blincoe, Paul Charles, Dennis Lehane, Maxim Jakubowski** and **John Foster**.

Ray Lowry: INK
1 899344 21 7 – Metric demy-quarto paperback original, £9

A unique collection of strips, single frame cartoons and word-play from well-known rock 'n' roll cartoonist Lowry, drawn from a career spanning 30 years of contributions to periodicals as diverse as Oz, The Observer, Punch, The Guardian, The Big Issue, The Times, The Face and NME. Each section is introduced by the author, recognised as one of Britain's most original, trenchant and uncompromising satirists, and many contributions are original and unpublished.

Maxim Jakubowski: THE STATE OF MONTANA
1 899344 43 8 half-C-format paperback original £5

Despite the title, as the novels opening line proclaims: 'Montana had never been to Montana". An unusual and erotic portrait of a woman from the "King of the erotic thriller" (Crime Time magazine).

New titles from The Do-Not Press:

Miles Gibson: KINGDOM SWANN
1 899344 34 9 – B-format paperback, £6.50

Kingdom Swann, Victorian master of the epic nude painting turns to photography and finds himself recording the erotic fantasies of a generation through the eye of the camera. A disgraceful tale of murky morals and unbridled matrons in a world of Suffragettes, flying machines and the shadow of war.

"Gibson has few equals among his contemporaries" —Time Out

"Gibson writes with a nervous versatility that is often very funny and never lacks a life of its own, speaking the language of our times as convincingly as aerosol graffiti" —The Guardian

Miles Gibson: VINEGAR SOUP
1 899344 33 0 – B-format paperback, £6.50

Gilbert Firestone, fat and fifty, works in the kitchen of the Hercules Café and dreams of travel and adventure. When his wife drowns in a pan of soup he abandons the kitchen and takes his family to start a new life in a jungle hotel in Africa. But rain, pygmies and crazy chickens start to turn his dreams into nightmares. And then the enormous Charlotte arrives with her brothel on wheels. An epic romance of true love, travel and food…

"I was tremendously cheered to find a book as original and refreshing as this one. Required reading…" —The Literary Review

Geno Washington: THE BLOOD BROTHERS
ISBN 1 899344 44 6 – B-format paperback original, £6.50

Set in the recent past, this début adventure novel from celebrated '60s-soul superstar Geno Washington launches a Vietnam Vet into a series of dangerous dering-dos, that propel him from the jungles of South East Asia to the deserts of Mauritania. Told in fast-paced Afro-American LA street style, The Blood Brothers is a swaggering non-stop wham-bam of blood, guts, lust, love, lost friendships and betrayals.

Paul Charles: FOUNTAIN OF SORROW Bloodlines
1 899344 38 1– demy 8vo casebound, £15.00
1 899344 39 X – B-format paperback original, £6.50

Third in the increasingly popular Detective Inspector Christy Kennedy mystery series, set in the fashionable Camden Town and Primrose Hill area of north London. Two men are killed in bizarre circumstances; is there a connection between their deaths and if so, what is it? It's up to DI Kennedy and his team to discover the truth and stop to a dangerous killer. The suspects are many and varied: a traditional jobbing criminal, a successful rock group manager, and the mysterious Miss Black Lipstick, to name but three. As BBC Radio's Talking Music programme avowed: "If you enjoy Morse, you'll enjoy Kennedy."

Also available from The Do-Not Press

It's Not A Runner Bean by Mark Steel

ISBN 1 899344 12 8 — C-format paperback original, £5.99

'I've never liked Mark Steel and I thoroughly resent the high quality of this book.' — Jack Dee

The life of a Slightly Successful Comedian can include a night spent on bare floorboards next to a pyromaniac squatter in Newcastle, followed by a day in Chichester with someone so aristocratic, they speak without ever moving their lips.

From his standpoint behind the microphone, Mark Steel is in the perfect position to view all human existence. Which is why this book — like his act, broadcasts and series' — is opinionated, passionate, and extremely funny. It even gets around to explaining the line (screamed at him by an Eighties yuppy): 'It's not a runner bean…' — which is another story.

'Hugely funny…' — Time Out

'A terrific book. I have never read any other book about comedy written by someone with a sense of humour.' — Jeremy Hardy, Socialist Review.

Elvis – The Novel by Robert Graham, Keith Baty

ISBN 1 899344 19 5 — C-format paperback original, £7

'Quite simply, the greatest music book ever written' — Mick Mercer, Melody Maker

The everyday tale of an imaginary superstar eccentric. The Presley neither his fans nor anyone else knew. First-born of triplets, he came from the backwoods of Tennessee. Driven by a burning ambition to sing opera, Fate sidetracked him into creating Rock 'n' roll.

His classic movie, Driving A Sportscar Down To A Beach In Hawaii didn't win the Oscar he yearned for, but The Beatles revived his flagging spirits, and he stunned the world with a guest appearance in Batman.

Further shockingly momentous events have led him to the peaceful, contented lifestyle he enjoys today.

'Books like this are few and far between.' — Charles Shaar Murray, NME

The Users by Brian Case

ISBN 1 899344 05 5 — C-format paperback, £5.99

The welcome return of Brian Case's brilliantly original '60s cult classic.

'A remarkable debut' — Anthony Burgess

'Why Case's spiky first novel from 1968 should have languished for nearly thirty years without a reprint must be one of the enigmas of modern publishing. Mercilessly funny and swaggeringly self-conscious, it could almost be a template for an early Martin Amis.' — Sunday Times.

Charlie's Choice: The First Charlie Muffin Omnibus by Brian Freemantle – Charlie Muffin; Clap Hands, Here Comes Charlie; The Inscrutable Charlie Muffin

ISBN I 899344 26 8, C-format paperback, £9

Charlie Muffin is not everybody's idea of the ideal espionage agent. Dishevelled, cantankerous and disrespectful, he refuses to play by the Establishment's rules. Charlie's axiom is to screw anyone from anywhere to avoid it happening to him. But it's not long before he finds himself offered up as an unwilling sacrifice by a disgraced Department, desperate to win points in a ruthless Cold War. Now for the first time, the first three Charlie Muffin books are collected together in one volume. 'Charlie is a marvellous creation' – Daily Mail

Song of the Suburbs by Simon Skinner

ISBN I 899 344 37 3 – B-format paperback original, £5

Born in a suburban English New Town and with a family constantly on the move (Essex to Kent to New York to the South of France to Surrey), who can wonder that Slim Manti feels rootless with a burning desire to take fun where he can find it? His solution is to keep on moving. And move he does: from girl to girl, town to town and country to country. He criss-crosses Europe looking for inspiration, circumnavigates America searching for a girl and drives to Tintagel for Arthur's Stone… Sometimes brutal, often hilarious, Song of the Suburbs is a Road Novel with a difference.

Head Injuries by Conrad Williams

ISBN I 899 344 36 5 – B-format paperback original, £5

It's winter and the English seaside town of Morecambe is dead. David knows exactly how it feels. Empty for as long as he can remember, he depends too much on a past filled with the excitements of drink, drugs and cold sex. The friends that sustained him then – Helen and Seamus – are here now and together they aim to pinpoint the source of the violence that has suddenly exploded into their lives. Soon to be a major film.

The Long Snake Tattoo by Frank Downes

ISBN I 899 344 35 7 – B-format paperback original, £5

Ted Hamilton's new job as night porter at the down-at-heel Eagle Hotel propels him into a world of seedy nocturnal goings-on and bizarre characters. These range from the pompous and near-efficient Mr Butterthwaite to bigoted old soldier Harry, via Claudia the harassed chambermaid and Alf Speed, a removals man with a penchant for uninvited naps in strange beds.
But then Ted begins to notice that something sinister is lurking beneath the surface

The Do-Not Press
Fiercely Independent Publishing

Keep in touch with what's happening at the cutting edge of independent British publishing.

Join The Do-Not Press Information Service and receive advance information of all our new titles, as well as news of events and launches in your area, and the occasional free gift and special offer.

Simply send your name and address to:
The Do-Not Press (Dept. CR)
PO Box 4215
London
SE23 2QD
or email us: thedonotpress@zoo.co.uk

There is no obligation to purchase and
no salesman will call.

Visit our regularly-updated web site:
http://www.thedonotpress.co.uk

Mail Order

All our titles are available from good bookshops, or (in case of difficulty) direct from The Do-Not Press at the address above. There is no charge for post and packing.
(NB: A postman may call.)